ANOTHER
Summer

A Wentworth Cove Novel: Book 1

Rebecca Stevenson

ISBN: 153512640X
ISBN-13: 978-1535126403

Dedication

To Jim, my husband and best friend, who never stopped encouraging me and believing I could do this

To Julie, my daughter, who helped me create a catalog-writing, aspiring-novelist hero, and who lovingly let me know what thirtysomethings would (and wouldn't) say

Contents

Chapter One

Wending her way through the unfamiliar serpentine streets of Wentworth Cove, Maine, Tracy Ratcliffe followed the directions she'd received in the mail, turned onto Old Sea Pines Road, and soon located the cottage that would be her sanctuary for the month of July.

Grayson Cottage was smaller but more charming than she'd imagined: a butter yellow clapboard with white trim, window boxes full of ruby red geraniums, and pink and white dahlias lining a curved stone walkway from the street to the front door. As instructed by the leasing agent, Tracy fished the key from one of the window boxes, unlocked the door, and stepped into the past.

Turning left from the living room filled with overstuffed chairs and a sofa covered in a floral chintz, she walked through the blue and white kitchen, entered the first of the two tiny bedrooms, and dropped her bag on the vintage ivory chenille bedspread that covered the double bed, her eyes surveying the room. The rooms in the cottage were small but adequate for a month, she decided.

1

Tracy had come here to get away from the city, and as she opened a window, the sounds and smells of small town New England reminded her just how far from Boston she actually was. The laughter of children playing nearby resounded in her ears, and the summer smell of freshly cut grass spoke of a village that was more vegetation than concrete, brick, and glass.

She hadn't wanted to take a vacation from her job as a literary agent, but her mother had insisted and had made Wentworth Cove sound so appealing that workaholic Tracy had taken the leap and asked for a month off.

For ten years, she'd been a full-fledged member of Boston's rat race. Having never married, and having no real interests other than work to consume her time, she spent ten to twelve hours a day pursuing writers—in a professional sense.

Although Tracy and her mother had developed an entirely satisfying friendship after her turbulent teen years, it was her father who had shown her the world at its best. All her life they had done everything together: explored secret trails, watched sunsets, read poetry, sailed. Kenneth Ratcliffe had so filled Tracy's life with beauty and companionship that she had no need, and no time for that matter, for boyfriends, much to the chagrin of some of Boston's most sought-after bachelors. When her dad died unexpectedly of a massive heart attack two weeks after her graduation from Boston College, Tracy felt an emptiness that neither her mother nor any of her friends could fill.

So she sought fulfillment from work. She immersed herself in words, the words her dad had treasured and devoted his life to. As a much-loved professor of English Literature at Harvard University, Dr. Ratcliffe had been on intimate terms with Austen, Maugham, Tolkien and Bronte. Tracy longed to be, too, but somehow teaching didn't appeal to her. So she turned her attention to discovering potential Austens, Maughams, Tolkiens, and Brontes.

But she had done it. After months of prodding from her mother, she'd left Boston with all of its hustle and bustle behind for a month and hoped she hadn't made a colossal mistake.

She retrieved her other bag from the car and began unpacking. A little concerned about what she was going to do for an entire month without manuscripts to read, she'd thrown in a couple of novels, but she would save them for later. After putting her clothes away in the antique oak armoire that served as a closet for the bedroom, food was uppermost on her mind. Her growling stomach reminded her that she hadn't eaten breakfast before she left Boston, so she set out for the market she'd passed a mile or two down the road, her eyes soaking in the quiet beauty of the village.

The sunlight glinted through the canopy of oaks and maples, and Tracy imagined how glorious they would be in the fall with their red, orange, and yellow leaves. The other houses along the way were larger than Grayson Cottage, and she wondered about the people who occupied them. Were they locals or summer people? How many of them would she meet during her month here? Did they contain happy families—families that took vacations together to see lighthouses and build sandcastles and sail and swim in the ocean?

Carson's Market was an understated blend of old-world charm and modern efficiency. Shelves extending from floor to ceiling contained artfully arranged bottles, cans, and boxes of food, from mundane to exotic. But cooking wasn't something Tracy enjoyed at home, and it certainly wasn't her idea of a vacation, so she opted for some easy-to-prepare items: frozen pizza, cereal, milk, coffee, bread, and lunchmeat.

As she was unloading the groceries back at the cottage, a knock at the front door startled Tracy. Not knowing a soul in Wentworth Cove, she certainly wasn't expecting guests. Her mother had spent a couple of months in this sleepy little village before Tracy was born while her father was studying at Oxford for the summer. As Laura had talked about it, Tracy noticed something about her mother she'd never seen before. What was it? A wistfulness maybe? She had obviously enjoyed the summer she'd spent here. She said it would be a place where Tracy could completely relax, as there wasn't much to do except walk the rocky coast and take in sunsets. Tracy hadn't enjoyed a sunset to its fullest since her dad's death. It would be nice to rediscover some of the joy she'd felt in her youth.

Another knock brought Tracy back to the present, and she opened the door to a woman—about the same age as her mother—dark hair pulled back at the nape of her neck, olive skin, and eyes of the most indeterminate light hazel Tracy had ever seen.

"Hi. I'm Kate Norsworthy. Saw your car and remembered hearing that someone would be staying in Grayson Cottage for the month of July, so I came to see if there's anything you need. I live in the blue house two doors down."

"I'm Tracy Ratcliffe. Just here for a month away from the city. Can't think of anything I need right now except...maybe... " She paused. What did she need? Time away from people? But Kate was being kind, and Tracy didn't want to be a total recluse while she was in Wentworth Cove. "Except maybe directions to the beach," she said finally. The beach. Any beach. The thought of sand, surf, and seaweed triggered so many memories. Memories that were lurking just under the surface and waiting to be set free.

"You're in luck. It's an easy walk from here. Keep going down Old Sea Pines Road for about a quarter of a mile, turn left on Shoreline, and it's another quarter mile or so."

Kate paused, took a small step back, and squinted a little. "Have you ever been to Wentworth Cove before?"

"No, this is my first time."

"I don't know why —" Kate stopped for a minute to scrutinize Tracy more closely. "—But you look familiar."

Tracy smiled at that statement, something she'd never heard before. With her light blonde hair, perpetually tan skin, and deep-set, velvet-brown eyes, people usually said she had an almost exotic and unusual look rather than a familiar one.

Kate didn't press the matter, though. "Well, if you need anything, just pop down to my house. I work at my son's art gallery on Harbor Road between noon and two every day. Other than that, I'm usually home and would love some company."

"Thank you," Tracy replied. "Did you say your son owns an art gallery? I used to love going to art galleries with my dad."

"Used to?"

"Dad passed away about ten years ago." Even though some time had passed, the memory still felt raw every time she had to tell someone. People had said that time would heal the wound, and although it partially had, some of the hurt and loneliness lingered. *Do you ever recover from losing someone you loved so much? Do you ever quit wondering why God took a good man and left so many bad ones?* Tracy had asked herself that many times.

"I'm sorry." It was everyone's stock response, but the sincerity in Kate's voice was apparent.

Why did Tracy already feel comfortable with this woman she'd known for approximately five minutes? Something about Kate's gentle demeanor had a calming effect on Tracy's Type-A personality.

"I'm sorry. I should have invited you in. Would you…" Tracy stepped back, opening the door wider.

"No. No, thanks. I just wanted to welcome you to Wentworth Cove, but you probably need to get settled in, so I'll leave you to it. I hope to see you again soon."

"Same here, and thank you for stopping by."

When Kate was gone, Tracy made herself a ham and cheese sandwich and walked out into the backyard. *What am I going to do here for a whole month? This could have been a mistake.*

But thinking about Kate's small-town friendliness once again put her at ease, and she made plans to visit the art gallery first thing in the morning.

She didn't set an alarm clock and slept until the first rays of sunshine bathed her with beams. Feeling the warmth of the morning sun on her face took Tracy back to her childhood when her mother would wake her gently by touching her face and saying, "Morning, Sunshine. Do you want a glass of sunshine juice?" Sunshine juice. Tracy needed orange juice like some people needed coffee to get them out of bed in the mornings, but she had forgotten to pick some up at the market yesterday. Oh well. She could tend to that today. What else did she have to do?

The art gallery. Kate's son's gallery. Tracy wondered what time it opened and glanced at her watch lying on the bedside table. Eight-thirty. When was the last time she'd slept until eight-thirty? She'd formed the habit of rising early, even on weekends, from so many days of getting up at six to get ready for a long commute from her home in the Brighton area of Boston to Smithson Literary Agency downtown. The windows were still open, and the salt sea air had acted like a sleeping pill. Despite the sounds of birds outside the window, she'd slept without waking for nine and a half hours. Tracy couldn't believe it. She had forgotten how good a long sleep could feel.

Surely the gallery would be open by the time she could have some cereal, shower, and walk to Harbor Road. Tracy had promised herself that she would walk when and where she could on this vacation. This might as well be an invigorating vacation as well as a relaxing one.

After drying her long, straight hair, she pulled it into a ponytail. Why should she spend time putting on makeup and curling her hair? After all, she wasn't trying to impress anyone here.

The sunshine was glorious as Tracy set out for the art gallery. Had Kate mentioned the name of her son's gallery? She wondered if it was the only one on Harbor Road.

The azure sky contained only a few sprinklings of fluffy white cumulus clouds, and the air had a tinge of Maine coolness—just enough to make a sweatshirt feel good over her khaki shorts.

Tracy didn't have to wonder long about being able to find the right gallery. As soon as she got a little way down Harbor Road, she saw the sign: Norsworthy Art Gallery. It had an enticing look, with beautiful paintings in the windows and red and tan striped awnings to shade them from the morning sun. She had driven right past the gallery on the way to the cottage but was so intent on following the map she'd missed this charming shop.

Walking in, she was captivated not only by the beauty of the gallery but also the warm atmosphere. Clearly,

someone much like Kate Norsworthy herself had
decorated this place. The aura invited her to come in and
feel at home.

The teenage girl sitting behind the desk glanced up
from her book and welcomed Tracy. "Hi. Is there anything
in particular I can help you find?"

"No, thank you. I just came in to look." Tracy glanced
around the gallery, amazed at the talent she saw displayed
on the walls and panels.

"Make yourself at home, and if there are any questions
you need answered, I'll try. This is my dad's gallery, but
I've been working here since I was twelve, so I know quite
a bit about the artists and the works we have on display."

So this was Kate's granddaughter. Tracy was not
surprised. Same dark hair and olive skin, same haunting
hazel eyes. Same friendliness.

"I met your grandmother yesterday. She told me about
this place and suggested that I come in and look around."
The girl's eyes widened, and she seemed to perk up at this
revelation.

"Oh, that's Gram all right. She likes to meet anyone
who's new in Wentworth Cove. She's Dad's best
advertisement for the gallery. Did you come for the
summer?"

"No. I rented Grayson Cottage for a month. It's a
couple of doors down from your grandmother."

"Yeah, I know where that is. Tim Grayson is a friend
of mine. The cottage belonged to his grandmother. She
passed away last summer, and this is the first time they've
rented it. It's been kind of hard on Tim. He and his
grandmother were very close."

Tracy was content and comfortable at Grayson Cottage
and enjoyed hearing a little of its history. She knew that
cottages in New England were often passed down from
one generation to the next and were kept in families, so
she wasn't surprised by this news. But for some reason,
she was glad to know that the place she was staying had

been enjoyed—and was still owned and loved—by a family. "Please tell him I'll take very good care of his grandmother's house while I'm here. It's lovely."

"I will. He'll be glad to hear that. As I said, make yourself at home. There are more paintings and a few sculptures upstairs, too. Oh, I forgot to tell you—my name's Jessica. What's yours?"

"Tracy. Nice to meet you, Jessica. You're as friendly as your grandmother."

"Thanks. Gram is a special lady." Jessica beamed. "She'll be here in a couple of hours. She always takes over at twelve so we can go to lunch. But just look around and have a good visit in Wentworth Cove."

"Thanks. I have a feeling I will."

The paintings captivated her. The Norsworthys obviously had an eye for good art. No amateurs here. Landscapes, seascapes, portraits—most with a New England look. Winslow Homer would have felt right at home. Lighthouses, ships, sailboats, coastlines, harbors—many of them took Tracy back to childhood memories of her dad, memories of sailing and lighthouse tours, making sandcastles, and looking for shells when the tide went out.

Upstairs were more paintings and some striking sculptures. She wandered around for a few minutes before noticing a balcony behind a pair of open French doors. What could she see of the area from up here? When she finally ventured out onto the balcony, she was surprised to find a man, obviously a Norsworthy judging by his coloring and his looks, sitting at a wicker table and working on a laptop computer. Could this be Jessica's father? It must be, she thought. The family resemblance was apparent. He looked too young, though—thirty at most. Maybe Jessica was younger than she looked; maybe he was older than he looked.

The man glanced up from whatever he was doing when Tracy walked out. "I'm sorry," she said. "I didn't mean to interrupt. I was looking at the paintings up here, saw the deck, and thought maybe I could see the coast from here."

"You can," he said as he turned back to his laptop. Not quite as friendly as the rest of his family. If this was his gallery, Tracy could see why he let his daughter and his mother run it. He didn't exactly fit the welcoming atmosphere she'd felt so far. She turned, walked back inside and down the stairs. When she reached the bottom, Jessica was talking to a young couple, obviously tourists, and Tracy was able to leave without being noticed.

Chapter Two

Glancing up and down Harbor Road to see if there was anything else she should explore, Tracy's eye lighted on a sign that read Down East Diner, Home of the Cove's Best Clam Chowder. She would be the judge of that. She'd vowed to eat a bowl of New England clam chowder at every restaurant she patronized while in Maine, and although it was only ten till eleven, she felt herself drawn to the restaurant.

Tracy walked in, saw the crowded room, and glanced at her watch again. Maybe she had looked at it wrong a few minutes ago. No, she was right. It wasn't even eleven o'clock yet, but this place was full. After finding a small table in the corner, she ordered a bowl of chowder.

The waitress was a short, plump pixie of a lady with curly, silver hair. Something she asked Tracy when she served her chowder had a familiar ring to it. "You've been to Wentworth Cove before, haven't you?" *The same question twice in two days. Do I really look that ordinary to be mistaken for someone else? If not, why do two people here think they've seen me before?*

11

"No, I haven't. This is my first time here," Tracy responded. "But that's the second time in two days I've heard that. Maybe I just have a face that looks familiar."

"No, it's not that. I can't really put my finger on it, but…" she paused and her forehead wrinkled as she pondered how to explain it. "It's just that…well, there's this portrait. Never mind. Impossible. It was painted too many years ago. Sorry I mentioned it. Enjoy your chowder and your stay here. And let me know if you need anything else."

"I will. Thank you." But as Tracy turned her attention to her clam chowder, she couldn't shake those words: "There's this portrait." What portrait? Where? And did it have something to do with the reason Kate had asked if she had been here before?

The sign outside was possibly not an exaggeration. She'd eaten a lot of clam chowder, but this was some of the best she had ever tasted. The jury was still out, though. It was only her second day in Wentworth Cove.

By the time Tracy had walked back to the cottage, she was feeling a little antsy. She could venture down to the beach. No, she would save the beach for later. Maybe this was a good time for a little reading. Sunlight from a small bay window bathed the room as she reclined on a chintz-covered sofa and picked up the Agatha Christie mystery from the dark mahogany coffee table.

The next thing she knew, she was waking up on the sofa with an open book lying across her legs. She checked her watch. It was four-thirty. How much had she read before falling asleep? Page fifteen. She hadn't been this relaxed for a long time. She never took naps in Boston.

The beach beckoned her then, so she put on comfortable walking shoes and headed down Old Sea Pines Road. It wasn't far at all, and she was enjoying all this walking, something she didn't do much at home except on a treadmill. The sea breeze felt good on her face, and the air tasted of salt and summer. Tracy had always loved the sights, smells and sounds of the ocean.

The tide was out, so she wandered up and down the beach, breathing in the almost-forgotten smell of seaweed and looking for seashells. Not having much luck in the seashell department, she had decided to make her way back toward the village when she saw him again, propped up with his back against a rock, open laptop resting precariously on his legs. He seemed lost in whatever he was working on. Completely absorbed. Since he'd been anything but friendly earlier in the day, Tracy wasn't eager for him to see her. If this was Jessica's dad, the friendliness gene must have skipped a generation.

Just then he looked up, and Tracy was sure he had seen her. But just as quickly, he looked back down again. No hello, no smile, no nod, no sign of recognition whatsoever.

Well, now that really was rude. I know he saw me, and how could he not recognize me as the person who interrupted him on the deck of the gallery this morning?

Turning and sprinting back to the house, she told herself it really didn't matter. After all, he was married. Even if he was about the best looking guy she'd run across in a very long time, he was definitely off limits.

After eating, she settled down in her pajamas and slippers and devoured the rest of her novel. One of the side effects of being a literary agent was the bad habit she'd developed of reading too fast. She told herself to slow down and enjoy this one, savor every word. After all, this one was purely for pleasure. Maybe she wasn't quite that relaxed yet.

The next morning was overcast, and a New England chill had invaded the cottage. Not cool enough to light a fire in the fireplace, but definitely too brisk for shorts. She decided this day was going to call for jeans and a sweater.

Since she hadn't seen Kate yesterday and she had invited Tracy to come over anytime, she decided to pay her a visit and tell her about seeing the art gallery and meeting her granddaughter.

Knocking lightly, she called out, "Kate, it's Tracy from Grayson Cottage."

"Come on in. I'm glad you came by," Kate said, holding the door open. "How's your vacation so far?" She was even more striking than Tracy remembered. Today her shoulder-length hair was down, and wearing jeans and a white cable-stitched sweater, she looked even more like Jessica. She almost appeared young enough to be her mother instead of her grandmother.

"Very relaxing. I'm sleeping well and getting in some pleasure reading, which I've wanted to do for a long time. I came over to tell you that I visited the art gallery and met your granddaughter."

"Oh, you met Jessica. She's the apple of my eye. A real sweetheart, that one."

Kate pulled out a maple, ladder-back kitchen chair and Tracy sat down. She decided not to ask Kate about the guy with the laptop. No need to pry. "Yes, she's very friendly. And the gallery was enticing. Beautiful. Did you have a hand in decorating it?"

"No, my son and daughter-in-law did that all by themselves. Jessica's mother teaches third grade in our local elementary school, but in the summer she helps out in the gallery. My son is really the one who knows art. He had an appreciation for it at an early age, and we encouraged his interest by taking him to art galleries when he was small."

"Well, it seems to have paid off. Where does he find all the paintings and sculptures? Are the artists local?"

"Many of them are. In fact, some of them live right here in Wentworth Cove. I'm sorry, Tracy. I haven't been a very good hostess. I had just made a pot of coffee before you got here. Won't you join me?"

Sitting in Kate's warm kitchen, Tracy decided she'd come to the right place to spend her month away from Boston. She didn't know the reason yet, couldn't put her finger on it, but something told her she was supposed to be here. Kate's genuineness? Maybe. But she had a curious feeling it was more than that.

"Sounds wonderful," she responded. "I didn't exactly anticipate this weather. In fact, I was going to ask you if there's a clothing store here. I packed some sweaters and sweatshirts, but a light jacket would feel good today, especially if I plan to do a lot of walking."

"We don't have one here in the village, but there's an outlet you'd probably like five miles away in Kennebunkport. Moose Creek Outfitters. In fact, I just happen to have a catalog. You can look through it, and if you find something you like, I'd be glad to take you over there this afternoon. I need to go into town and stop by the library anyway. Of course, I'll be at the shop until two, but any time after that. Have you done any exploring besides the art gallery? There are so many fun shops here in our little village."

Tracy wrapped her hands around the steaming cup of coffee Kate had poured for her. "I had a delicious bowl of clam chowder at Down East Diner yesterday and walked the beach for about an hour. That's all. My mother wanted me to come here to relax. I know I needed to get away, but I'm not the kind of person who can sit around very long. I'm going to have to find some trails to explore, I guess."

"I'll do some thinking. Not much going on around here, but maybe I can come up with something to keep you busy."

As they sat silently sipping their coffee, Tracy felt comfortable in Kate's cozy kitchen. Conversation was nice, but the ability to sit with someone without exchanging words might be even nicer, Tracy thought.

After a minute or two, Kate broke the silence. "Tell me about your mother, Tracy. You mentioned that she was the one who encouraged you to come to Wentworth Cove."

"She's a librarian at one of the branches in Boston, the Brighton branch. She hasn't remarried since my dad died, hasn't even dated, actually. I imagine she thinks she couldn't find anyone quite like him—and she's right. My dad was almost perfect." Tracy paused, thinking about her dad. After ten years, she still had trouble believing he was gone. "Mom and I get along better now than we ever have. We've grown much closer in the last few years. I guess we need each other more now."

"I can certainly understand her being hesitant to date after a very satisfying marriage. I've dated only one man since my George died, and only for a short time. I'm happy with my independence." That was the first time Kate had mentioned a husband, and Tracy had wondered if she was widowed or divorced since she apparently wasn't married. Mystery solved.

"I think my mother feels the same way. I doubt she'll ever remarry." Tracy rose from her chair and pushed it in. "I've taken up enough of your time this morning. Thanks for the coffee—and for making an outsider feel so welcome here."

"You *are* welcome here. It's always nice to have new faces in the summer. There aren't as many here this year as usual. Take that catalog, and let me know if you want to go into town with me this afternoon. I'll be leaving around three."

"Sure, I'd love to go. I don't think I have any pressing appointments today."

Kate laughed her hearty, infectious laugh. What a wonderful friend she was going to be this month.

"Great. I'll pick you up at three then."

So, the unfriendly guy with the laptop has a wife and she's a teacher, Tracy thought on the way back. *She must have carried all the conversations in that household until Jessica learned to talk.*

As soon as she got back to the cottage, Tracy sat down on the couch and began thumbing through the catalog Kate had given her. She was right. The clothes were the casual and simple style Tracy liked. She found a lightweight jacket she thought would be just right for days like today and read the information about it. It told an entire story in one paragraph, apparently written by someone who had an unusually excessive amount of time on his or her hands and a very vivid imagination. Tracy kept turning the pages, reading some of the most creative descriptions she'd ever seen, thinking she would like to meet the person who could make these clothes sound so appealing.

By the time three o'clock rolled around, Tracy was more than ready to get out of the house. Riding into Kennebunkport in Kate's Jeep, she heard a running history of the area. *The Herringtons live here; their ancestors were the first family in Wentworth Cove. The Chamberlains live over there; their family has been in that house since 1875. The Weilers live there; Miriam Weiler is mayor of Wentworth Cove, and her husband Isaac is our newspaper editor.*

The Ratcliffes usually vacationed on Cape Cod. This terrain was so different. The Cape had miles of silvery sand beaches dotted only with an occasional patch of sea grass. The coast here was more majestic as the waves crashed violently against craggy rocks. Tracy had been to Maine once or twice before but never for any length of time. Reminiscing about family vacations made her think of her mother. She should call her soon and tell her how much she was already enjoying this time away from work… and thank her for suggesting Wentworth Cove.

They arrived at the Kennebunk library first, and Tracy decided to go in with Kate. She could look around and check out their selection of fiction in case her next novel read as fast as the first one. The library took her by surprise. For a relatively small structure, it had an outstanding selection of not only fiction but also nonfiction, books on CD, DVDs, magazines, and a bank of eight computers on one side of the room. Kate introduced her to the librarian, a distinguished-looking man, probably in his late fifties or early sixties-- tall, silver-haired, handsome in a cardigan-sweater, plaid-shirt sort of way.

"John, this is Tracy. She's spending a month at Grayson Cottage, and I'm showing her the big city of Kennebunk."

John studied Tracy's face a little longer than she thought necessary before he said, "I'm very pleased to meet you, Tracy."

"I was just admiring your library," Tracy said. "You've done a lot with a small amount of space here." He was still looking at her in an odd way, almost as if he thought he had seen her before, too. It was becoming an epidemic, and, to tell the truth, it was beginning to make her feel a little uneasy.

"Well, thank you," he said finally. "This library is sort of my home, actually. I've been the librarian here for—let's see—how long has it been, Kate? About thirty-five years, I suppose."

"Has it been that long? Don't remind me, John. I don't feel a day over thirty-five myself, do you?"

"I have my moments, but usually I feel every one of my fifty-nine years."

"I guess we'd better be about our business, hadn't we, Tracy? I'm taking Tracy over to Moose Creek Outfitters. She didn't anticipate this cold spell in July."

"You come to us from somewhere in the South?" John inquired. "You don't sound like most of the Southerners who summer here."

"No, I'm from Boston, but I haven't taken a vacation in so long, I guess I'm just not a very adept packer." Did she see a noticeable change in John's face when she mentioned Boston, or was she reading things into people's expressions now?

"I see. Well, I won't keep you two any longer. I hope you enjoy your stay, and if you get too bored, remember you're always welcome here. I'll instruct my staff to check out books to you if I'm not here when you come in. We usually lend only to locals, but I'll make an exception in your case, since you're a friend of Kate. We're not as big as what you're used to in Boston, but I think you'll be able to find something readable here."

"If you count quality instead of quantity, I'd say you have a very nice library here. And I know something about libraries. My mother is a librarian, too."

"That so?" John mused after what seemed like a very long time. Tracy didn't quite know how to read him yet, but something about him—and his library—was intriguing. She decided to devour her second novel as fast as she had the first and pay him another visit to replenish her reading supply.

"Take care, John," called Kate on their way out. "And thanks for saving that new Bradford novel for me."

John stepped from behind the checkout desk and walked them out. "Sure, any time." He waved as they drove off, but Tracy noticed that, for whatever reason, his entire demeanor had changed from the time they walked in to when they left. He looked...what? Almost shaken. Tracy wasn't sure what to make of it.

Back in the Jeep, Tracy didn't know whether to mention her feelings to Kate. She certainly didn't want her to think she was paranoid if this was all her imagination. On the other hand, she'd been getting some unsettling vibes since she arrived. She opted not to say anything, yet at least.

"John's very nice and not bad looking either," Tracy teased Kate.

"That's all true," she answered, "but we're just friends. All we'll ever be is just friends. I'll be honest with you, Tracy. John is the man I was telling you about, the only one I've had even the slightest feelings for since George died, but nothing came of it, and nothing ever will. And that's all right with me. I wouldn't want to ruin a special friendship."

"John seems like a nice man. I'm sorry it didn't work out for you two."

"It's the proverbial long story," Kate began. "I'll shorten it and fill you in on the way back to Wentworth Cove. My life is an open book. No secrets from anyone, and I might as well let you in on it. The whole town knows anyway," she said, smiling.

By now, Tracy was properly curious.

Kate pulled the car into the parking lot at Moose Creek Outfitters, and as they walked in, Tracy looked around thinking of the catalog Kate had lent her earlier, the one with little snippets of some of the most enjoyable and imaginative prose she'd ever read. The clothes and household decorations were nice, but not that special. How could someone see a plain brown sweater or an ordinary black knee-length dress and get inspired to write an entire story? Some of her published writers couldn't write description this compelling.

Tracy found the jacket she'd located in the catalog, told Kate she was ready, and got in line to pay. She could come back and look around later—there would be plenty of time—and she didn't want to inconvenience Kate in any way. Besides, she was eager to hear about the romance that never was.

Chapter Three

Tracy and Kate drove in comfortable silence for a while before Kate started talking.

"When George was killed in an airplane crash—he was flying one of his clients back to Bangor in our small plane and something happened to the engine—I'm not sure what. Well, anyway, I pretty much fell apart. We had lived a Cleaver-type life until then—a storybook romance—a wonderful family, the home of our dreams in the most beautiful place on earth. I'm a little prejudiced about Wentworth Cove," Kate smiled.

"John was the one who brought me back to life. Not at first. It took quite a while, but he persevered, made me see the sky again, made me laugh again. We'd been friends since childhood. Then gradually the relationship started changing, for me at least. And for him, too, in a way. But he could never give me his whole heart. He had lost it many years before and had never been able to get it back to give it to anyone else."

"I'm sorry," Tracy said, sensing that she had been through an ordeal, but she wasn't one to want pity.

"Thank you. But don't feel bad about what happened between John and me. That was for the best. As I said before, I really do enjoy my independence, and we have a beautiful friendship, which I treasure."

Tracy was curious about the man she had just met. "Do you know anything about John's earlier romance? I'm betting there's quite a story there."

"I know a little, but I don't remember her name. It was a summer romance, but she was married. I think John had fallen in love before he knew there was a husband somewhere—hadn't even thought of that as a possibility. By that time, there was no turning back for him."

It couldn't possibly be. That was too long ago. "How long ago was that, Kate?" Tracy managed to get out.

"A very long time. Thirty years or so, I suppose. John had only been at the library a couple of years. George and I were already married." Apparently, Kate was oblivious to Tracy's sudden feeling of anxiety. She kept talking.

"The saddest part of it was that one of our local artists painted a portrait of the young woman walking along the shore—she was beautiful—blonde hair and the most gorgeous brown eyes—coloring the same as yours actually—and it hung in the gallery—long before my son owned it, of course—for about a year. John couldn't stand it, and he finally bought it. I suppose he still has it at his house, although it doesn't hang in his living room. Of course, I would never ask him about it."

Tracy was having trouble speaking. For the first time in her life, she couldn't find the right words. A portrait? The one the waitress at Down East Diner had mentioned? The waitress who apparently thought she looked like the woman in the portrait.

She wanted to ask more questions, to find out more about the married woman who had stolen John's heart. Was this the reason a couple of people had thought she looked familiar? Two people who were old enough to remember the portrait and who had lived here when it hung in the gallery? The reason John's demeanor seemed to change when she mentioned being from Boston... and especially when she mentioned that her mother was a librarian?

And yet, she didn't want to know, so she decided to change the subject. Denial, maybe? If Kate thought the change abrupt, she didn't seem to mind. They talked about the weather, the terrain, and the history of the area until they arrived in front of Grayson Cottage.

"Here we are. I'm glad you went into town with me today."

"Thank you for taking me. I'm glad to know there's a library that close by. I'm down to my last novel."

Once inside, Tracy remembered she had resolved to call her mother. Did she really want to now? Would she be tempted to start asking questions? She resigned to put all that she'd learned today in the back of her mind. It *was* denial, but that seemed to be the only way she could cope. Anyway, she wasn't ready to know the truth—afraid of what she might find out. Her mind had been racing to all kinds of possibilities she didn't want to consider.

Proud of herself for waiting three days to use it, she took her cell phone out of her bag and dialed Laura's number.

"Hello."

"Hi, Mom. Just thought I'd let you know I'm doing what you told me to do."

"What's that?"

"Relaxing, of course."

"That must have been someone else. I would never interfere in your life. You know that, Tracy." Tracy just smiled at this obvious bit of sarcasm.

"Anyway," Tracy continued, "I'm glad you suggested this. I didn't realize how much I needed to get away from the office and from the Boston rat race. The first night here I slept for nine hours straight."

"Wonderful. I'm sure you needed it. Have you met anyone interesting?"

"A really nice lady two doors down—and her granddaughter. Her son owns an art gallery here." Tracy was determined not to mention John.

"I remember going to an art gallery the summer I was there. Wonder if it's the same one. Have you ventured into Kennebunk, yet?" A perfect time to mention the library… to mention meeting John. But she couldn't. Not yet. There was still an uneasiness about the situation in the back of her mind.

"Yes. Kate, the lady who lives down the street, took me in to buy a jacket. I don't know what I was thinking when I packed. It was overcast and cold today, and all I packed were light sweaters and sweatshirts. The jacket felt good."

"Unfortunately, you don't have much practice packing."

"You've got me there, Mom. But I think this will be the beginning of more time away from the office. It feels good here. The salt air is invigorating. I've only walked along the shore once, but I'm thinking about going out again this evening."

"I'm glad you're enjoying your time there. I had a feeling you would. I know I loved my summer there. It's a special time and a special place I'll never forget." Tracy paced the room, unable to respond for a moment, but ready to bring this conversation to an end.

"Well, I'll let you go," she managed to say.

"Love you, Trace."

"I love you, too, Mom, and I'll call again in a few days. Oh, how's Molly?"

"She's spoiled. But then you already knew that, didn't you?"

Molly was their beloved Yorkshire terrier, as much Tracy's as Laura's and as much Laura's as Tracy's. She was at Tracy's townhome about as much as she was at Laura's house. They laughed and called it "joint custody."

"I surely do know that. And she'll probably be worse when I get home."

"Ha! We both know whose fault it is. But let's don't argue about that now. Anything on the guy horizon?"

"Mom!"

"Well, a mom's got to ask."

"As a matter of fact, I did meet someone, sort of. He's gorgeous, the quintessential 'tall, dark and handsome,' but he's unfriendly—and I think he's married." She'd said it before thinking. *Tracy, stay away from that subject.*

"It doesn't sound promising, then," Laura laughed. "Let me know if anything interesting happens."

"Don't hold your breath."

"I won't. I know my daughter and I love you just the way you are. Don't worry about my not being a grandmother, although all my friends are. Don't fret your pretty little head about it."

"Don't worry. I won't give it a second thought. I'll call again soon."

"Be careful… Sorry. I know you're thirty-one, but it's a mom thing."

"Bye. Give Moll a kiss for me."

"I will. Have fun."

Tracy put the phone down and decided she would have to stay extremely busy to keep from thinking the unthinkable. She knew her mom and dad had had a few disagreements, but basically they had been happy. She was sure of that. In fact, one of her friends had jokingly referred to them as "lovebirds." It simply was not possible that her mother had had a summer fling. She would walk on the beach and put that thought completely out of her mind.

Chapter Four

Putting on her new jacket, Tracy stepped out into the cool, humid air. A great time for a walk along the oceanfront—about an hour before sunset, though there would be no sunset tonight for her viewing because of the cloud cover.

Meandering down the rocky New England coastline, she began taking deep breaths of the seaweed-scented air, and as she did, her mind began to clear. This was Tracy's medicine, a poultice for her aching soul. The sea was working its magic on her again for the first time in several years.

She hadn't walked far when she saw in the distance a young couple approaching, hand in hand. She had begun to think maybe she was missing out on something by not having a serious relationship, and seeing those two brought the thought to the forefront of her mind once again. There had been Craig a couple of years ago, and although they dated for more than two years, Tracy knew it would never be anything serious—whether he did or not. It ended for just that reason; he wanted "serious" more than she did.

She could think of a couple of others her mom would have loved as a son-in-law, but Tracy kept telling Laura that she was not the one who would have to live with them, and they were not right for her. Laura finally acquiesced and they dropped the subject. Temporarily anyway.

As the couple drew nearer, she recognized the girl as Jessica. Jessica apparently recognized Tracy, too, because she started waving and called out, "Hi, Tracy!"

She met me once and remembers my name. I'm impressed.

"Hi, Jessica. I didn't expect to see anyone I knew out here, especially since I've been here only three days."

"Tracy, this is Tim Grayson. You know—I told you about him when you were in the gallery. You're staying in his grandmother's house."

"I'm glad to meet you, Tim," Tracy said. He was quite a contrast to Jessica with his light blonde hair and dark blue eyes. She wondered how old they both were. Couldn't be more than sixteen or seventeen.

"You, too," replied Tim.

Tracy decided to venture into uncharted waters. "Jessica, I think I saw your dad during my stroll along the beach yesterday. He was working on his laptop, just like the time I saw him in the art gallery."

"Oh, that's not possible. Dad's out of town for a few days. He went to an art show in Bar Harbor day before yesterday and won't be back until tomorrow. Mom, Gram, and I are holding down the fort by ourselves until he gets back."

Well, one mystery was solved. Sort of. "I just assumed it was your dad since I saw him on the deck upstairs in the gallery working on his laptop."

"If he looked like Gram and me and had a laptop attached to the ends of his fingers, that was my uncle Nathan. He lives in the other part of the house that's not the gallery."

"Oh, well, that explains it. I thought he looked too young to be your dad, but I saw the family resemblance." *And the family resemblance serves him well,* Tracy thought. *If only he resembled Kate and Jessica in other ways, too. Like maybe their friendliness?*

"Yeah. I look more like him than I do my dad. Dad has brown eyes like my grandfather did," Jessica explained.

Tracy had jumped to the wrong conclusion in this instance, and she could only hope she was doing the same thing about another matter that kept gnawing at her.

Deciding to change the subject before she got too inquisitive, she turned her attention to Tim. "I'm enjoying staying in your grandmother's home. It's comfortable and convenient to the shops in Wentworth Cove and the beach."

"Cool." Tim was not a man of many words, Tracy concluded, but he had a smile that produced the most irresistible dimple she had seen in a long time, and he seemed to be polite. He and Jessica were still holding hands, their fingers tightly interlocked.

"I'll let you two get back to your walk. It was nice to run into you, though."

"You, too. I'll see you around," replied Jessica as she and Tim continued to make their way down the coastline. Tracy turned to watch for a moment. Yes, it might be nice to have someone to walk with, someone to sail with, someone to watch sunsets with, someone to share her joys and her fears with. Her mother would be proud of her for thinking like that. Laura had always been an incurable romantic.

Some of the rocks were slippery, but Tracy navigated them carefully and managed to enjoy her time, even though the wind was biting cold by now. Who would have thought it would be this cold in July? Thoughts of a fire in the fireplace, crackling and smelling of cedar, propelled her back toward Old Sea Pines Road and Grayson Cottage.

Apparently, the Graysons had anticipated this cold weather even in the summer. Wood had already been laid for a fire, and a box of fireplace matches lay nearby. Maybe Tracy had stayed too busy in Boston to think much about the weather. At home she was usually either at work, at the gym, or in her townhome. Unless she was walking Molly or heading to the train stop, she rarely ventured outside.

Soon she was sitting in a large, floral overstuffed chair with a ham sandwich in one hand, a book in the other, and a delightful fire popping and crackling in front of her.

Wednesday morning she decided to visit some of the other shops in Wentworth Cove. Since walking had served her well so far, she would save her car for trips into Kennebunkport and on up the coast if she decided to venture as far as Camden or Bar Harbor. She remembered a family vacation all the way up into Nova Scotia when she was about twelve or thirteen and had some photos at home of the trip. She'd always been captivated by those pictures because of the irresistible appeal of the scenery, so different from Boston, and Cape Cod for that matter. The views from Mount Battie and Cadillac Mountain. The rustic charm of the small villages of Damariscotta, Belfast and Wiscasset. Red barns with hand-painted signs advertising antiques for sale.

Tracy had never picked up any orange juice and needed to replenish some supplies, so her first stop in town was Carson's Market. As she was walking up the front walkway toward the house after getting the groceries, a voice called out, "Let me give you a hand." She turned and recognized Tim Grayson walking toward her, his arms outstretched to take her bag of groceries. "Came to see if you needed some more firewood."

"Thanks. That would be nice in case it gets as cold again as it was last night."

He set the sack on the kitchen table. "I'll be right back," he called, as he rushed out.

By the time she'd finished putting the groceries away, he was back with an armload of firewood. Not as chatty as Jessica, but much more so than her uncle Nathan, Tim was certainly a gentleman, especially for a sixteen- or seventeen-year-old boy.

Always up for a challenge, Tracy decided to try to get a conversation started with him. "Jessica says you and your grandmother were close," she began.

"Yes, we were." That was all. Try again.

"I hope you don't mind that I'm staying in her cottage."

"No, I'm glad because you seem to like it." One more time.

"Oh, I do. It's tastefully furnished and very comfortable, and that fire last night felt really good."

"Well, I'd better go. I have to be at work in a few minutes," Tim said, turning and walking toward the door.

"Oh? Where do you work? Here in Wentworth Cove?"

"I work at Wentworth Rentals. We rent bicycles, motorbikes and sailboats."

Sailboats. How Tracy would love to go out on one, but she was definitely not a solo sailor. She'd always sailed with someone else, someone more experienced. Usually her dad.

It was, she supposed, the end of that conversation, so she thanked him once again for the firewood, and he was gone, leaving Tracy alone with her memories.

There was no TV in the cottage, but that was something she wouldn't miss. Tracy had never been much of a TV watcher, probably because she was the progeny of a librarian and an English professor. But there was a small radio in the bedroom, and Tracy decided to see if she could find a station with some music she liked. She located a suitable station and set about putting together a salad for lunch. After a few minutes the music stopped, and Tracy heard an announcer say something about the Fourth of July.

The Fourth of July? It hadn't entered her mind, but if Tracy's calculations were right, since she'd arrived on Sunday, June 30, tomorrow would be a holiday. She wondered what kinds of festivities Wentworth Cove would have. Watching fireworks had always been a favorite Independence Day activity for the family, and after her dad died, Laura and Tracy had continued the tradition. *Maybe Mom will go somewhere with some friends tomorrow night,* Tracy hoped.

After eating her salad, Tracy ventured into town to see the shops that were still waiting patiently for her perusal. As she wandered down Harbor Road and walked by the art gallery, she turned her head just in time to see a tall, striking blonde in a red pantsuit talking with what appeared to be the same two customers Jessica had been helping when she made her hasty exit on Monday. Could this possibly be Jessica's mother? Jessica certainly didn't look much like her, and Tracy had been wrong before, but it seemed likely since Kate hadn't mentioned anyone else who worked there.

On down the street she noticed a candy store, a candle shop, and a store that sold ship models. She wandered into each one and looked around for a few minutes. Glancing across the street, her eyes fell on a sign that read: Bernard's Books and Collectibles—New, Used and Rare First Editions. Like a powerful magnet, those words pulled her across the street and into the shop.

Walking in, Tracy took a deep breath and filled her lungs with that same wonderful, musty smell she remembered from her dad's library at home. What was it about dark wooden shelves filled with books that made her heart skip a beat? Looking toward the back, she saw a young woman on a ladder looking for something on one of the upper shelves, and it reminded her of that scene in *Funny Face* when Fred Astaire walks into the bookstore and sees Audrey Hepburn for the first time. She looked a little like Audrey Hepburn, in fact, slim with her dark brown hair pulled back into a ponytail at the nape of her neck.

When she saw Tracy, she asked if there was anything in particular she was looking for. "Not really, just browsing," Tracy answered.

"Welcome to Bernard's. Feel free to look around as long as you like, and let me know if you need help finding something."

Never had Tracy seen so many rare first editions in one location. Whoever this Bernard was, he had a goldmine in books in this shop. Tracy wandered around for what must have been ten or fifteen minutes, drinking in the distinct aura that only old literary works could give a room. The dark plank floor and polished oak paneling added to the atmosphere, too, giving it even more of an old-world charm.

Several people had come and gone since Tracy walked in, but she was the only one in the shop now and decided to inquire about one of the first editions she thought her dad would have liked to receive as a gift. It was times like these that made her miss him the most, enjoying alone what they used to take pleasure in together. *How he would have loved this beautiful place!*

As Tracy and Maggie talked about first editions and favorite authors, she discovered Ladder Girl knew a lot about the books she tended. Her name was Maggie Culwell, and she was a native of Wentworth Cove. Tracy bought a used copy of *The Ponder Heart* to round out her Eudora Welty collection and decided it was time for lunch. She still had tasted clam chowder only once since arriving, and it was time to try again.

"Who makes the best clam chowder in Wentworth Cove?" she asked Maggie.

"Down East Diner claims to, but I think the chowder at Lobster Bistro around the corner on South Street is better," she responded, adding, "I was just about to close the shop for an hour and take a lunch break. Would you like to go with me?"

Although Tracy was used to eating alone and didn't mind it, she thought Maggie's company would be nice. They had talked easily, and maybe Maggie could tell Tracy what people their age did in Wentworth Cove for fun. At least Tracy thought she was near her age and noticed she wasn't wearing a wedding ring.

Maggie put up a sign that read "Closed for lunch. Back at 12:30," locked the door, and they walked around the corner to Lobster Bistro. They sat in a booth and both ordered a salad and a cup of clam chowder. Their tastes, in books and food at least, seemed to run along the same lines.

"How long have you been in town?" Maggie asked as they sipped their sodas.

"Only three and a half days. I arrived Sunday afternoon."

"Where are you staying?"

"Grayson Cottage on Old Sea Pines Road. Do you know where that is?"

"Yeah. Mrs. Grayson, who used to own that house, was my senior English teacher. She was the one who instilled in me a love of books. She was so happy that I was working at Bernard's, though she always thought I should go to college, but my parents couldn't afford it, and I wasn't a good enough student to get any scholarships. She died about a year ago."

"I've met her grandson, Tim. I heard that her death was rather hard on him."

"On the whole family—the whole town, actually. She was special to so many people here. Had taught many of them senior English, and she had taught some of her most recent students' parents, too."

Deciding to change the subject and get right to the point, Tracy asked, "What do people around here do for fun? You're the first person close to my age that I've met." She couldn't count Laptop Guy; they hadn't exactly had an engaging conversation.

"Well, it depends on what you like to do, but there's really not much in Wentworth Cove other than family and church stuff. You'll have to go into Kennebunk or Portland to meet many people our age who are single. Portland's a little farther, but it has a pretty thriving night life," Maggie offered. "Since tomorrow's the Fourth of July, all the shops'll be closed, and there'll be a parade down Harbor Road. It starts at ten. Then tomorrow night we'll have fireworks on the beach. I watch both of those every year on the Fourth. Would you like to go with me tomorrow?"

Although Tracy had enjoyed Kate's company, she was eager for someone to talk to who was closer to her own age and jumped at the offer. "Love to. Thanks."

"Great. Let's meet in front of the shop at a quarter till ten. That'll give us plenty of time to get a good spot. The street's usually not crowed right there."

"I'll be there." By then their salads and chowder had arrived, and they ate in silence for a while.

"This chowder is delicious. Thanks for recommending this place and for asking me to join you." Tracy made a mental note that Down East Diner still lived up to its claim to have the best, though.

"I'm glad you like it," Maggie replied. "It's nice to have someone new to eat lunch with. Bernard and I usually close the shop and go to lunch together, but he's not exactly my idea of a great companion—a really nice person to work for, but a little old for me."

"How old is he?" Tracy asked.

"Seventy-five."

"Oh, I see," she said, laughing.

They walked back to the bookstore together, and Tracy continued her trek toward the cottage. She was just inquisitive enough about John to finish her second novel so she'd have an excuse to drive into Kennebunk and visit the library on Friday. Intense curiosity fueled her desire as much as, if not more than, the need for some new books to read. There was a thought she couldn't get out of the back of her mind, and not knowing was something she'd never been able to live with. If she were a cat, she would have been dead by now. That whole curiosity thing.

The rest of the afternoon was spent curled up in that wonderful chintz-covered chair with the latest Grisham novel. Not very scholarly reading, but that was, after all, what she was getting away from when she left Boston.

She woke up early the next morning looking forward to spending part of the day with Maggie. She was instantly likable, and Tracy was especially happy to have met someone who wasn't the age of either her mother or the teenage daughter of one of the men she'd recently dated.

Donning her denim shorts and a long-sleeved white polo shirt, she decided this time to add a touch of makeup and curl the ends of her hair, just in case. *You never know. Maybe Maggie has a friend*, she mused as she applied mascara to her already long, thick lashes, and she realized she was thinking more like her mother every day.

Chapter Five

Arriving a few minutes early, Tracy started looking for Maggie. People were already lining up, and she glanced around to see if anyone looked familiar. Many families were there with young children, and some had even brought their dogs. Her thoughts immediately turned to Molly and how much she would enjoy being in this crowd; she was a real "people" dog. Small sons and daughters were perched on their fathers' wide shoulders so they could have a bird's-eye view of the parade. The scene made Tracy realize how different this lifestyle was from the one she was used to, and she thought about the possible benefits of growing up in a small town as opposed to a big city. All she'd ever known was city life, and she'd always considered herself a city girl. Tall buildings, mass transportation, sounds of horns honking impatiently in the sometimes bumper-to-bumper traffic.

As she was pondering how conducive small town life was for rearing children, Maggie walked up and they began chatting easily, as though they'd known each other much longer than one day. They talked about the weather—sixty-five degrees and sunny—perfect for outdoor festivities, a few of the people she saw on the other side of the street, and Boston. Maggie had been there only once many years ago and wanted to know more about it. As Tracy told her about the commuter train she took into town, the traffic, the downtown area where she worked, and the shopping malls, the scene before her took on an almost mythical quality. It was so foreign from what she was used to.

They soon heard sounds of a high school band stepping to a Sousa medley, and the parade was underway. After the band came floats from local businesses, trucks filled with Boy Scouts and Girl Scouts, a bevy of antique cars, and a group of red-nosed clowns throwing wrapped candy into the crowd, delighting the children. When the next float passed by, she thought her eyes were surely deceiving her. She'd seen him only twice, but there was no mistaking that face. Nathan Norsworthy was sitting on a float in the middle of a group of boys and girls who couldn't have been more than four or five years old. Mr. Personality himself. With a group of children. What was that all about?

She must have been staring because when his eyes met hers, he waved and Tracy froze. So he *did* recognize her. But why had he decided to be friendly now? During a parade.

Then Tracy realized Maggie was waving, too, and it made much more sense. He was waving at Maggie, not her. Even though Tracy still didn't like him, she felt a little disappointed when the realization hit her.

"Isn't that the brother of the guy who owns the art gallery across the street?" she ventured.

"Yeah. That's Nathan Norsworthy. He's a year older than me, but I've known him since I was in first grade," Maggie replied.

"I thought I recognized him from seeing him in the gallery a couple of days ago. What's he doing with all those children? He doesn't seem like the type." Well, *that* was an understatement.

"Oh, Nathan loves two things: kids and writing. His laptop is his best friend, but the boys and girls in his YMCA day camp group run a close second. He even keeps in touch with them after all the summer day camps are over. Sometimes he takes them sailing or fishing, especially the ones whose parents don't have much time to spend with them."

What a revelation this was to Tracy. She had definitely judged this guy wrong if he spent time with children whose parents had no time for them.

"I'm impressed. When I saw him the other day, I got the impression he wasn't very friendly."

"Well, he *is* kind of quiet, at least until you get to know him, but he's a really great guy."

Maggie invited Tracy to her house after the parade to meet her parents and younger sister, Annie. They all quizzed her about Boston, especially Annie who'd just graduated from high school and desperately wanted to go to Boston, get a job, and be a big city girl. If Tracy hadn't known Maggie and Annie were sisters, she wouldn't have guessed it. Annie's face didn't have that sweet innocence that Maggie's had, and Tracy thought she was trying a little too hard to look older than her eighteen years.

"What's it like to live in Boston, Tracy? I always thought it would be so stimulating to live in a big city. What's the traffic like? Are there just tons and tons of shops and restaurants so that you never have to go to the same ones twice? Oh, that would be so much fun!" As Annie spoke, asking questions faster than Tracy could answer them, she grew increasingly animated.

"Well, it does have its advantages, but as I've seen since coming to Wentworth Cove, it has its disadvantages, too. Traffic, for one. I don't drive much in Boston, but when I do, I usually end up wishing I'd taken the train."

"But the restaurants. Oh, if I had that many to choose from, I'd never get bored."

"You might think that, Annie, but you can get bored anywhere. I work long hours, but if I didn't, I don't know how I would spend my time there."

"I can think of a thousand ways. The first one being meeting new guys. Can you imagine growing up in a place like this and knowing the same people your whole life? Sometimes I think I'll go crazy before I can get out of here."

Maggie chimed in. "Oh, Annie. Wentworth Cove isn't so bad. It has its good points, and you'd be happier if you'd think of those instead of always putting it down."

"Well, you can spend your life thinking about the good points of living in a small town, but I prefer to set my sights a little higher."

Hoping to bring the conversation to a more pleasant topic, Maggie asked, "Tracy, tell us about your job. You're a literary agent, right? That sounds kind of exciting. Is it?"

Tracy told them about her job at Smithson Literary, and they all seemed impressed. She sensed that none of them had spent much time away from Wentworth Cove.

Before leaving to go back to the cottage, she made plans to meet Maggie and Annie at the shore just before dark to watch the fireworks from Kennebunkport. When Maggie said the whole town would be there, Tracy found herself wishing they would just happen to run into Nathan and that Maggie would introduce them. For some reason, she wanted a new beginning with him. Erase the two times she'd seen him before and forget that he was rather rude on the deck of the art gallery. Chalk it up to the fact that he was engrossed in his writing.

Was it the fact that he was a writer that had intensified her attraction to him? That he was good with children? Or could it have anything to do with his being the best looking unattached guy Tracy had seen in a very long time?

Being a literary agent and seeing writers come and go every day, she knew it surely wasn't that he was a writer; although, she wondered what he was so intent on writing. And she had certainly known plenty of guys who liked kids. Craig had let her know he wanted no fewer than five when he got married. Come to think of it, it wasn't long after that conversation that she quit seeing him. Something about Nathan Norsworthy, though, had her interested enough to start seriously considering what she was going to wear to the fireworks show on the beach. A fashion decision was approaching, and for the first time in a while Tracy found herself missing her best friend, Gina Lundsford, who always knew the perfect outfit and accessories for any outing.

She spent the rest of the afternoon reading and napping. Tracy hadn't thought about John Strong for a while, but a vague worry still nagged at her, and she decided she had to go back to Kennebunk on Friday. What she could find out from going into the library and checking out some books, she didn't know, but she did know that putting the thought completely out of her mind was out of the question. She'd already tried and failed miserably.

How would she handle finding out her mother had had an affair with this man who must have been very handsome thirty years ago? She wished she could see the portrait Kate said he had at his house, but she couldn't exactly go up to him and say, "Pardon me, but I hear you have a portrait of a woman I think might be my mother. Do you mind if I take a look?"

As conflicted as her feelings were, she didn't want to bring up old wounds. John had feelings, too, and apparently whoever this woman was, if what Kate said was true, knowing her during the summer of 1982 had affected him greatly.

Turning her attention to tonight, she searched the closet for exactly the right outfit...just in case. Tracy finally settled on her newest jeans and a hot pink silk sweater. Most of the people would probably be dressed in red, white and blue; hot pink would stand out from the crowd. Just the right touch, she decided. Gina would be proud of her.

Chapter Six

The late evening sky was brushed with broad strokes of purple and gold, and the beach was swarming with people when Tracy arrived. She wondered how many were tourists and how many were locals. Children scampered around waving miniature American flags, and parents had brought folding chairs and blankets to spread out on the beach. It was a snapshot of Americana that could have come straight out of a Norman Rockwell painting.

One family in particular made Tracy especially nostalgic. A little girl, about four or five years old, was holding her father's hand, pulling him and begging him to walk with her along the shore so the waves could hit her legs. How many times had Tracy and her father walked along the shore hand in hand? How many times had he given in to her pleading even though he was tired and would rather have been sitting on the beach under a huge umbrella with a good book?

She'd been looking for Maggie and Annie for about fifteen minutes. Just as she was about to turn and walk in

the other direction, Jessica tapped her on the shoulder.
"Hi," she said, her other hand firmly enclosed in Tim's, as
it had been the last time Tracy had seen them together.

"Well, hello," Tracy responded. "It looks like the whole
town's here tonight."

"And then some. People from Augusta and other
inland towns come out here to see the fireworks.
Something about seeing them light up and reflect off the
ocean, I guess. This is the only place I've ever seen them,
but a lot of people say it's the best."

"Well, I'm glad I came then."

"Are you here with someone?" Tim asked.

"I'm meeting a new friend. Her name's Maggie, and she
works at Bernard's Books. She has a sister named Annie
who's supposed to come, too," Tracy replied.

"Oh, I know them. Maggie and Annie Culwell.
Maggie's a friend of Uncle Nathan's. In fact, I think she's
had a crush on him for years...and we know Annie, too,
don't we?" Jessica threw the slightest glance Tim's way. "If
you don't find them, you can always sit with us. We have a
blanket over there." She pointed to an area near the
water's edge.

"Thanks. If I don't find them in a few minutes, I'll
come on over there."

Just then Annie walked up. "Hi, Tim. Hi, Jess. I didn't
know you knew Tracy."

"Jessica's grandmother was the first person I met when
I arrived, and I'm staying in Tim's grandmother's cottage. I
met Jessica at the art gallery Monday," Tracy explained.

"Oh, I see," Annie said after a long silence. Did Tracy
sense tension in the air? Jessica and Tim said goodbye and
walked away without saying anything to Annie. *I wonder
what's going on with the three of them,* Tracy thought.

"Maggie's over there." Annie motioned to the left. "We
split up since we weren't having any luck finding you
together." Annie didn't seem to have the same softness
about her that Tracy had sensed in Maggie.

They walked up the shoreline and located Maggie who was talking to a short, rotund, balding man with bright blue eyes, bushy eyebrows and rosy cheeks. "Tracy, this is Bernard, my boss. This is Tracy Ratcliffe. I met her yesterday when she came in the bookstore."

"It's nice to meet you, Mr..." She couldn't remember if Maggie had mentioned a last name yesterday or not.

"Bernard, please. The pleasure is mine, young lady. I hope you enjoyed our little shop. I trust Maggie helped you find what you were looking for."

"Actually, I was just browsing. I'm a sucker for bookstores, but yours is especially nice," Tracy said sincerely.

"Thank you and do come in again. Are you new to Wentworth Cove or are you one of our summer people?"

"I'm just here for the month of July."

"Well, welcome. I'll let you young people do whatever it is young people do these days. I'm meeting my mother in about five minutes. She wouldn't miss the Independence Day fireworks for anything."

"His mother?" Tracy queried unbelievingly when Bernard was out of earshot. "How old did you say he is?"

"Bernard's seventy-five, and his mother is ninety-three. She's pretty spry, though. Still calls to remind him of things, and from what I hear, she beats everyone at Scrabble and works *The New York Times* crossword puzzles with a pen."

"Well, I'm impressed," Tracy laughed. "I can barely work them with a pencil."

"Maggie, there's Nathan," Annie interrupted. "Let's go over and say hi."

"No, Annie," Maggie said. "Let's leave him alone. If he wants to talk, he'll come over here."

"No, he won't. You know him. You know you'll have to be the one to talk to him first."

"Well, then, we just won't talk."

"That's your problem. That's why you're still single. I'll go talk to him then." Annie was not one to be deterred.

"Fine. You do that." Maggie was not one to be bullied by her little sister, either.

Annie was off. Tracy hadn't seen Nathan yet and wondered what he looked like standing up. All three times she'd seen him he was sitting, and she was curious about how tall he was. She'd told her mother he was tall, dark and handsome, but she wasn't really sure about the "tall" part yet. Jessica said that Maggie had had a crush on him for years, and Tracy wondered if anything had ever come of it.

In a couple of minutes, she glanced to the right just in time to see Annie and Nathan walking toward them. Tracy was right about the height. He appeared to be about six-two and was more handsome than she remembered in denim shorts, sandals, and a sweater the exact same pale gray-green as his eyes. All of a sudden she found herself wondering if her hair still looked all right and if her lipstick was still on, but she forced herself to keep her hands still. *This isn't like you, Tracy, caring about things like that. You don't even like this guy. He's rude… remember?*

"Nathan's not here with anyone, so I invited him to hang out with us. That's okay, isn't it?" Annie asked.

"Of course it is," Maggie answered, smiling. "Hi, Nathan. This is Tracy Ratcliffe. She's spending a month in Wentworth Cove, staying in Grayson Cottage."

"Hello," Nathan said.

That was all. Hello. *You're not going to get off that easily.* "We've already met, sort of," Tracy began. "Remember, I walked onto the balcony at the gallery to look at the scenery, and you were writing? That was a few days ago, though."

"I remember. And I saw you walking on the beach later that day."

"You were writing then, too. I wasn't sure you saw me since you didn't say anything." Tracy was glad to be able to get in that little dig.

"It's about time for the fireworks to start," Annie interrupted. "Let's find a good place and put the blanket down."

Their conversation was over, and Tracy found herself wondering if Annie had intentionally ended it. It was obvious she was trying to set him up with Maggie... or did she want him for herself? She was barely out of high school, but Tracy had a feeling that with a girl like Annie that small detail didn't matter. She seemed in many ways older than Maggie, although she was ten years younger.

They found one of the few flat places on the sand that wasn't taken and spread out the blanket. Maggie, Annie and Tracy sat down first. Did Nathan deliberately sit by her, or was there just more room on her side of the blanket? *Don't read anything into that, Tracy.*

Maggie seemed unusually quiet since Nathan had joined them, but silence was not a problem with Annie around.

"Tracy works in Boston, Nathan. I'm thinking about going to Boston University this fall myself. I think it would be fun to live in a big city. If I moved to Boston, would you come to see me?"

Before Nathan could answer Annie's question, the fireworks started. They watched in silence as the scarlet, emerald, indigo, silver, and gold explosions lit up the night sky. Tracy couldn't help but think of how different the Boston sky was. With all the lights in the city, it was never dark enough for the stars to show as brightly as they did over the ocean. The fireworks were brighter and more vibrant here, too. No wonder people came from Augusta.

After a while, Annie had apparently had about all the silence she could stand. "Where are we going after this is over?"

"Nothing's open. It's the Fourth... remember, Annie?" Maggie inserted.

"I'd be glad to have everyone over, but I don't have much food in the house right now," Tracy offered.

"That's OK," Maggie said. "Annie and I ate just before we came out here. We'd love to come over, wouldn't we, Annie?"

"Sure. Nathan, are you coming, too? You're invited, isn't he, Tracy?"

"Of course he is." *Of course he is?* At this point Tracy's feelings about Nathan were conflicted. Did she want to get to know him, or would it be better to cut it off right here before she got involved, before she lost her head over this gorgeous guy?

"I could go by my house and pick up some things," Nathan offered. "I made some crab cakes and lobster rolls after the parade today."

"You cook, too?" *What was I thinking saying that? Watch yourself, Tracy. You don't want to sound too impressed.*

"A little." Nathan waved his hand in the air as if dismissing the topic, and Tracy thought he seemed a little embarrassed.

"Don't be modest, Nathan. You were asking where you could get a good bowl of clam chowder, Tracy. Nathan makes the best clam chowder in Wentworth Cove. Better than Down East Diner or Lobster Bistro," Maggie said.

"Don't exaggerate, Maggie. Down East Diner wouldn't be happy if they heard you say that," he said. He was opening up, and Tracy sensed that maybe she'd jumped to the conclusion that he was rude too hastily. All of a sudden, she was silently thanking Annie for inviting him to join them. Still concerned with Jessica's revelation that Maggie was interested in him, Tracy wondered what their relationship really was. Obviously they were friends, but was that all? She didn't want to hurt Maggie in any way.

They watched the rest of the fireworks, inserting the appropriate "oohs" and "aahs" in the right places. When the grand finale was over, Tracy said, "It's settled then. Everyone over to my place. Well, my place for this month, anyway. Nathan, do you know where Grayson Cottage is?" As soon as the words were out of her mouth, she realized what a ridiculous question that was. He'd lived here all his life, and it was two doors down from his mother's house. Mrs. Grayson had probably been his senior English teacher, too.

He smiled. "I think I can find it, but I'll go pick up some food and drinks first."

Maggie, Annie, and Tracy rode back to the cottage in Maggie's car with Annie chattering all the way. She talked about the fireworks, her plans to go to Boston, and chided Maggie for not being friendlier to Nathan.

"You know, Maggie, if I can't have him for myself, at least I could have him as a brother-in-law. That is, if you'd do your part. Then I could look at his beautiful green eyes to my heart's content. I might not even move to Boston then."

"Annie," Maggie countered, "you go ahead and move to Boston. If anything were going to happen between Nathan and me, it would have happened long before now. You know we're just friends."

"Well, I'm not giving up. You know you've liked him forever, and he's not married yet, so who knows?"

By that time they'd reached the cottage, and Tracy was relieved. She was getting a little uncomfortable with the topic of conversation.

"Come on in," she said. "It's little, but it's cozy."

"So this is where Mrs. Grayson lived," Annie said, walking in and looking around, as if casing the joint. "I can't believe she retired before I was a senior, and I had to have Mrs. Nicholson for senior English. We didn't get along very well." Tracy wasn't all that surprised.

"I'm sure if she could have, she would have stayed just for you," Maggie teased. They got along remarkably well considering the fact that they were so different, Tracy thought.

Annie was chattering away about moving to Boston again when there was a knock on the door. Opening it, Tracy saw Nathan standing there with an armload of food and a pitcher of lemonade.

"I'm not a very good hostess, making you bring the food, but thanks for all this," she apologized.

"That's okay. I usually make too much anyway. It's hard to cook for one."

"I have that same problem, but I usually opt not to cook rather than cooking too much."

"I guess it's a creative outlet for me," he responded as they carried the food into the kitchen.

Thinking that she had her creative outlet in her work, Tracy wondered what he did to support himself. All she had ever seen him doing was writing. Could he be so good that he wrote for a living? Unless he had published under a pen name, Tracy was pretty certain that he didn't write novels. Not that she'd heard of every published novelist, but she was familiar with most of the names of those who could actually quit their day jobs.

Annie and Nathan sat in the living room talking while Maggie helped Tracy put together a salad. That was about all she had to offer in the way of food.

The weather was cool with just a hint of an ocean breeze blowing, so they decided to eat in the backyard. Nathan set up the folding lawn chairs while Annie got the plates and lemonade ready.

"I played in this yard when I was a kid," Nathan announced after they'd been eating for a couple of minutes. "I grew up on this street, just two houses down, in fact."

"I know," Tracy replied. "Your mother was the first person I met when I got here Sunday. She came over to welcome me, and Tuesday we drove to Kennebunkport together."

"Was she the one who told you about the art gallery?"

"As a matter of fact, she was. How'd you guess?"

"She's pretty proud of David and his accomplishments, and she never fails to show off the gallery to anyone who'll take her up on an invitation."

Did Tracy sense an undercurrent of sibling rivalry? "These crab cakes are delicious," she inserted as she forked another one off the plate. "Where'd you learn to make them?"

"Cooking just came naturally to me. I can't remember a time when I wasn't trying to help Mom in the kitchen. Though, I'm not sure she would call what I did helping. I probably made more work for her since I managed to mess up the kitchen quite easily but never could seem to get around to cleaning it up."

"I'm sure she appreciated it. My mom was happy if I even set foot in the kitchen during meal preparation. Cooking has never been one of my hobbies, as you can probably tell by the lack of food in the house."

"What do you like to do in your spare time?" Nathan asked. Tracy was surprised that the two of them were carrying the conversation without interruption, from Annie especially. What did she like to do? That was a good question, one she'd been thinking about a lot in the last few days.

"I read a lot, and I like to sail; although, I haven't done any sailing in quite a while."

Apparently, Annie had had all she could take of this two-way conversation. "Nathan, you never answered my question about whether you would come see me if I moved to Boston. Would you?"

"Sure, I would, Annie. When are you going?" he answered. Probably just to be nice, Tracy thought. She'd really misjudged him. He didn't seem rude at all now.

"If I can't get into Boston University, I'll probably go soon and try to get a job there. It would beat staying around here for the rest of my life," she said, turning to look pointedly at Maggie.

"Staying around here's not so bad, Annie," Maggie said. "I can think of worse things."

"Name one," Annie challenged.

"Driving in Boston traffic. I don't think I would like that."

"It is bad, Maggie. And don't even get me started on the lack of parking spaces once you get where you're going. I take the commuter train into the city so I don't have to drive in it. But the train has its own challenges, too."

"Where are you going to live?" Maggie, obviously the practical one, asked Annie.

"Tracy, I could stay with you until I could find a place of my own, couldn't I?" Not a shy bone in this girl's body, Tracy concluded. Pretty nervy, in fact. She wasn't exactly sure how to answer.

"Well…" she stalled.

"You can't just assume you can live with Tracy, and you shouldn't even mention it. She's only known you one day. Besides, she might have a roommate and not have room for you." It was apparent that this was not the first time Maggie had had to reel in her little sister. She should be on a short leash, this one.

After a few seconds, Tracy felt as though she should be the one to break the silence. "I don't have a roommate, but I have only one bedroom. I'll try to help you find a place, though. There are some apartment locater agencies that have roommate services. That's probably the route you should take since you don't know anyone there."

"That would be great. Of course, if I get into Boston U, I can live in a dorm, right?"

"Of course," Tracy answered.

"Then it's settled. I'll come down in August. Could I stay with you a few days just to check out the university and the job situation? I could sleep on your sofa."

"Sure. That would be fine." Tracy, feeling defeated, gave in, hoping Annie would change her mind before it became an issue.

Maggie was apparently uncomfortable with Annie's assertiveness and decided it was time for them to make their exit. "Let's go, Annie. It's getting late and I have to work tomorrow."

"I need to go, too," Nathan spoke up, as he stood and walked toward the door, "but thanks for letting me crash your party."

"Oh, I'm glad you came…and not just because you brought the food," Tracy said, smiling. *Definitely not just because you brought the food.*

"Bye, Maggie and Annie. I'll see you later."

Alone in the cottage, Tracy couldn't get her mind off Nathan. It was amazing how just a few hours had completely revolutionized her thinking about him. He was not at all the ogre she had first thought him to be. He was, on the other hand, extremely kind and patient with Annie, and Tracy was impressed that he took such an interest in children at the day camp. There was still an air of mystery about him and many unanswered questions. The next three weeks could be interesting.

Chapter Seven

The next morning Tracy remembered her resolve to go back to Kennebunk and to the library. She would check out some books, but she still hadn't decided how to learn more about John and his relationship with the woman in the painting. All her life she'd been told how much she looked like her mother. Maybe when he saw her again he would bring up the subject, and she wouldn't have to. Still not sure she wanted to know the truth, but positive she couldn't live with not knowing, she showered and dressed quickly, had a bowl of Raisin Bran and a glass of orange juice, and drove straight to the library.

Tracy saw John as soon as she walked in. He recognized her immediately. "Welcome to our little library again. Did you run out of reading material already?"

"Yes. I read too fast. I'm trying to slow down and savor each book, but it's difficult. I guess I'm too accustomed to the fast-paced life of Boston." Tracy thought maybe the mention of Boston would be a catalyst to turn the conversation toward the topic of her curiosity, but John didn't take the bait.

"Well," he said, "if you stay around here for any length of time, you'll learn how to slow down and enjoy life at a much slower pace. We don't get in much of a hurry. That's probably because there's not much to do after you finish what you *were* doing, so you might as well stay at it a little longer." Tracy was in a quandary. John Strong was likable, but she didn't want to like him. She didn't want to think favorably of the man who had possibly seduced her mother while her dad was away for the summer.

"Do you have any novel suggestions?"

"What kind of books do you like?"

"Usually something with at least a hint of suspense."

"Have you seen Jacqueline Fairchild's latest? I have it, and I don't believe it's checked out right now." He walked a few steps to the right where new releases were shelved. "Ah, here it is."

"I'll take it on your recommendation. Thank you. I'll just look around a little, too, and maybe I can find something else while I'm here."

"Of course, take your time. I have to leave for a couple of hours, but Ruth will be glad to help you check out when you're ready."

Since she hadn't come with a plan, Tracy was at a loss on how to dig more deeply into the mystery of who was in the painting that John had bought. Although she enjoyed reading suspense, this true-to-life drama that was unfolding in Maine was a little more than she had anticipated or hoped for. She thought it irrational to jump to conclusions, but still...the evidence seemed to be adding up to an inevitability that she didn't want to face. She thought she knew her mother well, but how much had she really tried to get to know her? Had she ever encouraged her to talk about things that were important to her? Had she really listened when her mother seemed inclined to talk about the past? Was something like this a part of her life that she would choose to share with Tracy?

Looking around a few more minutes and not finding anything else that captured her interest, Tracy decided to take only the book that John had recommended. Taking only one would give her a reason to come back to the library in case her courage grew in proportion to her curiosity.

As she drove back to Wentworth Cove, her thoughts went from John to Nathan and back to John again. It was amazing how much had happened in only five days—how much she had learned, how much she had yet to learn... about both men.

Trying to think about something less emotional, Tracy studied the scenery: sun-washed cottages and once-dilapidated mansions that had been lovingly restored to a state of splendor; peonies, snapdragons, zinnias, and anemones growing in lush abandon in many of the yards; stately trees and hedges that lent privacy where it was needed; winding woodland paths branching off from the highway tempting her to explore them.

Back at the cottage, she decided it was time to call her mother again since Laura was going to wait for Tracy to call her and would probably be wondering whether she'd met anyone "interesting." It would make her day to hear about how Tracy had misjudged Nathan and that they'd talked last night during and after the fireworks.

"Boston Public Library... Brighton Branch... Laura Ratcliffe speaking."

"Hi, Mom. Sorry to bother you at work, but I thought you'd be in bed last night when I got a chance to call."

"That's okay. We're not busy right now. How are you? Still having a relaxing vacation?"

"So far it's been just what Dr. Mom ordered."

"Good. Fill me in on some of the details—if there are any."

"Well, you're probably not interested in hearing about Nathan, so I'll skip that."

"Okay, I'll bite. Who's Nathan?"

"He's the gorgeous guy I told you about before, the son of the neighbor who was so nice to me when I first got here."

"The married one?"

"I was wrong about that. That's his brother who's married, the one who owns the art gallery. I haven't met him yet, but I did watch fireworks with Nathan and he came over to the cottage afterward. We ate lobster rolls and crab cakes." Tracy smiled, knowing how much her mom was enjoying hearing about a guy she might be interested in.

"Well, then I know it's serious. It would take someone very special to entice you to cook. And where did you learn to make lobster rolls and crab cakes? Have you turned over a new leaf?"

"Oh, I didn't do the cooking. He did. And before you get too excited about this, I should explain. We were with Maggie and Annie."

"And who are Maggie and Annie? Please don't be cruel and tell me that one of them is his fiancé. A mother can only take so much."

"No," Tracy laughed. "I heard from his niece that Maggie has had a crush on him for a long time, but she says they're just friends—and Annie is only eighteen. So as far as I know, he's a free agent."

"Sounds interesting. Keep me posted. What else have you been doing?"

Feeling a little braver than the last time they talked and deciding it was the only way she would ever be able to put this behind her, Tracy said, "I finished both of the novels I brought with me and drove into Kennebunk today and went to the library."

There was an even longer pause than Tracy expected before her mother said, "Tell me about the library. You know I'm always scouting other libraries for new ideas. Did you talk with any of the librarians?"

Take a deep breath, Tracy. "Yes, I met the head librarian. He's a friend of Kate Norsworthy. It's a really great library—not nicer than yours, of course, and not as large."

Another lengthy pause before Laura asked, "Did you get his name? I remember that library from thirty years ago when I spent some time in Wentworth Cove, and I seem to remember meeting the librarian. I wonder if it could be the same person after all these years."

"It must be because he said he'd been the librarian there for thirty-five years. His name is John Strong."

"John Strong... yes... I remember." Was Tracy mistaken, or was it a wistful tone she heard in her mother's voice? It wasn't what she wanted to hear. She wanted to hear her say she'd never met John before, that she must be thinking of someone else, that she'd never had any interest in a librarian named John Strong, that she had never loved anyone but Tracy's father. *Can you say that, Mom? Please?*

"Tracy? Are you there?"

"Yes... I... I'm here... How's Molly?"

"She's fine, but I took her out last night to watch fireworks with me, and they frightened her. Haven't we taken her before? I thought we had."

"Not that I remember. Is she okay now?"

"Sure. She's resilient. She misses you, though."

"Kiss her for me. I'd better let you get back to work. I'll call again soon."

"Yes. Do. Keep me posted about... What was his name?"

"I don't know who you're talking about."

"Nathan?"

"Don't get your hopes up. What can happen in a month?"

"You'd be surprised." This answer from Laura sent Tracy reeling. She didn't want to think her mother meant anything by it, but she couldn't help getting a sick feeling in the pit of her stomach.

"I have to go, Mom."

"Bye. Don't forget to call again soon."

"I won't. Bye."

Tracy turned her phone off and laid it on the table. *What do I do now?* She didn't want to keep thinking something that wasn't true, but how could she find out for sure? Kate would be her best bet. She remembered the painting and the woman who was in it. Tracy had a wallet-sized family picture in her purse of her mom, her dad, and her that was taken at her college graduation. *If I show that to Kate and start asking questions, she'll want to know why. What will I tell her? I'll have to be honest and tell her my concerns. I can't do it any other way. Although I haven't known her long, she seems like someone I can trust. She's so easy to talk to.*

Tracy spent the rest of Friday and the weekend by herself—reading, listening to music, walking along the shore, and thinking. As usual, when she was at the beach, her thoughts turned to her father. She supposed that was why she'd come to Maine this time instead of going back to Hyannis, Chatham, or Rockport. Too many memories there.

Monday morning her first stop was Kate's house. With the picture tucked away in her front jeans pocket, she'd decided to forge ahead with her plan to discover what really happened the summer of 1982 when her mother had spent two months in Wentworth Cove.

Tracy's light knock on the door brought Kate immediately.

"Hi, Tracy. It's good to see you. Come in." Kate opened the door wide, motioning her into the kitchen.

"How've you been?"

"I'm fine—been reading a lot—and I met some people, one of them being your son Nathan." Tracy surprised herself by feeling comfortable divulging this information to Kate. "He knows Maggie and Annie Culwell. They asked me to join them for the fireworks. Maggie introduced us, and he came to the cottage with them afterward. I was kind of embarrassed because he had to bring the food since I'm not much of a cook. He is, though. A good one, too. Did you teach him?"

"I guess you could say I gave him the opportunity to hone his natural talents, letting him shadow me in the kitchen and cleaning up his messes. I'm glad you had the opportunity to meet him. He's my pride and joy. Not as outgoing as David but much more sensitive and introspective. Each child has his own unique talents and characteristics, and I'm quite proud of both of them." Tracy wasn't surprised, but she was glad to hear that Kate valued both of her sons equally since she had gotten a different vibe from Nathan.

"I can see why. The crab cakes and lobster rolls were delicious."

"Sit down and stay a while, Tracy," Kate said, pulling out one of the kitchen chairs. "Can I get you a cup of coffee? What brings you out so early?"

"No, thanks. I had a cup before I came over. I wanted to talk to you about something, and if this isn't a good time, please let me know. I can come back later."

"No… no, this is as good a time as any. What was it you wanted to talk about? You've piqued my curiosity."

"You know, I think I will have another cup of coffee if you don't mind." Maybe a little caffeine boost would return the courage that seemed to be slipping away.

"Sure. My coffee always tastes better with a blueberry muffin, though. Won't you join me?"

"I really didn't come over for a free breakfast, but that does sound tempting. Thank you."

There was no other way for Tracy to go about this than to start at the beginning and explain her suspicions to Kate. She took a sip of the steaming coffee that Kate had put in front of her, set her cup down on the oak table and breathed in deeply. "Do you remember when we first met and you asked if I had ever been to Wentworth Cove before? You said I looked familiar."

"I remember quite well," she replied. "It's not every day that someone as attractive as you—with that exquisite combination of brown eyes, tan skin and light blonde hair—comes along, and for some reason your looks struck a familiar chord in me. I'm still not sure why." Kate had a puzzled look on her face. "But why do you ask?"

"Would you take a look at this picture and tell me if the woman in it looks familiar to you?" Tracy pulled the picture out of her pocket and laid it down on the table, careful to keep her father and herself covered with her hand.

"She looks like an older version of you. This must be your mother. She's lovely. I'm still not following your line of questioning, though. Kate looked thoroughly confused.

"Remember telling me about a painting that hung in the art gallery before it belonged to David? I hope I'm wrong, but I have reasons to think my mother might have been the young woman in that picture."

"You mean…" Kate paused, gradually drinking in the realization of what Tracy was saying. "You mean you think your mother is the woman John fell in love with?" Kate gently laid her hand on Tracy's, obviously empathetic to what she was feeling. "Tracy, I haven't seen the painting for many years now, but as I recall, the woman did look a lot like you. She was tall and slender with dark brown eyes and long, straight blond hair. I saw her in person a couple of times, but that was more than thirty years ago, and my memory of that time is vague. As I said before, George and I were already married, and David was about two or three. Why do you think that woman is your mother? I know you wouldn't jump to conclusions unless you had some very strong reasons."

"You're right, but unfortunately I do. In the first place, you're not the only person who has asked me if I have been here before. There was a waitress in Down East Diner, and…"

"John's sister is a waitress there. Was she kind of short with short, curly, silver hair?" Kate asked.

"Then that makes sense. She's probably seen the painting at his house." This was all becoming clearer to Tracy, and she didn't like the fact that it was. She had wanted to hear Kate say, "No, that woman couldn't have been your mother. She was a brunette." Or, "She was short and pudgy." Or something. Something to assure Tracy that her mother wasn't the woman whose portrait resided in John Strong's house. But that's not what she was saying. She was confirming Tracy's suspicions, and Tracy was feeling more and more like she might not really know her mother at all.

"Yes, I'm sure she has. Still not conclusive, though. What else is there?" The tenderness in Kate's voice assured her she'd come to the right person.

"The day we went to the library, and I met John…" Tracy's voice broke, revealing her pent up emotions. Not normally a crier, she felt on the verge of tears.

Sensing her anxiety, Kate said, "Take your time, honey. I have all the time in the world. I can always call David and tell him I can't come in today."

Tracy sat for a couple of minutes regaining her composure before continuing. "I sensed something in John when I mentioned that I was from Boston… and again when I revealed that my mother was a librarian. It wasn't anything he said, more like the way he said it."

"I didn't think John was exactly himself that day either, but I didn't really think anything about it then. But now…"

"That's not all, Kate. I called my mother a couple of days ago and told her about meeting the librarian at Kennebunk. She said she remembered him, so I know for sure that they have at least met."

"You know, Tracy, there are some things that should be left alone…and I'm thinking maybe this is one of them." Tracy knew there was wisdom in Kate's statement, but at the same time she knew she couldn't leave it alone. She couldn't quit asking questions until she knew for sure whether the woman John Strong fell in love with so many years before was her mother. Whether the woman in the hidden portrait was Laura Ratcliffe.

"I wish I could do that, but I don't think I can," Tracy said.

"Well, then, you must find out for sure before you mention it to either John or your mother."

"Would you remember her name? My mother's name is Laura."

Kate was quiet for a minute. "That was a long time ago, Tracy. I'm sorry. I wish I could tell you more."

Tracy's face fell as she knew she'd probably hit a stone wall in her investigation and that Kate wouldn't be able to help her solve the mystery.

After a moment Kate said, "Wait… I do remember something that might be helpful to you. I think I remember that the woman in the portrait rented a room from Nora Solomon. Nora still lives here. She's quite elderly though and quit renting rooms to summer people about fifteen or twenty years ago. It would be a long shot, but it might be worth a try if you would like to go see her. I'll go with you if you'd like."

"I think I *would* like that," Tracy said gratefully, relishing in this sliver of a possibility.

"I'll give Nora a call this afternoon and see if we can see her tomorrow. Is that too soon for you?"

"No, not at all. I'd like to get this over with as soon as possible. I've always been able to deal with things better if

I know for sure. It's the not knowing that eats at me. I'm afraid I won't be able to enjoy the rest of my vacation until this is settled one way or another."

"I want to help any way I can, Tracy." Kate wouldn't let her leave until she'd agreed to come for dinner that evening. She was having her family over and wanted Tracy to be a part of the festivities. Looking forward to seeing Nathan again and to meeting David and his wife, she was fairly easily persuaded.

Chapter Eight

Nora Solomon, Kate explained to Tracy on the way to her house, was in some ways considered the matriarch of Wentworth Cove. At ninety-three, she was by far the oldest resident of the village, and Tracy surmised that she must be Bernard's mother. Her hope was that Nora could help her put her fears to rest by telling her that it was not her mother who had stayed in Nora's home that summer but some other blonde woman who looked a lot like her. Someone named Susan or Karen or Linda.

They pulled up to Nora's house at ten-thirty on Tuesday morning, and when she greeted them at the door, she looked at least twenty years younger than her age. Tracy recalled what Maggie had told her about Nora playing Scrabble and working crossword puzzles with a pen instead of a pencil. Tracy thought it fortunate that she was still alive and alert enough to talk intelligently about the summer of 1982.

Kate introduced them, and Nora offered tea. It wasn't without trepidation that Tracy had come to Nora's house today. A cup of tea might be just the thing to calm the butterflies in her stomach before she got to the point of the visit. Nora poured with the dexterity of a much younger woman, obviously quite practiced at this gracious art.

"It's so nice to have someone over for tea that I hate to rush this, but I am curious about the reason for your call, Kate," Nora began.

"Nora, Tracy is spending a month here—she's in Virginia Grayson's house—and she has a question of some import to her. I told her you would be the one to ask. It's about a woman who might have rented a room from you about thirty years ago. Do you remember the woman whose portrait Samuel Jacks painted and had it hanging in the art gallery for so long before someone purchased it?"

"Of course, I remember," Nora said without missing a beat. "Beautiful woman. Probably the most attractive guest I had in the twenty or so years I rented out that room for the summer. One of the few I corresponded with when summer was over. Can't remember her name, though. I remember when Samuel came over to ask her if she would pose for him on the beach. That portrait was in the gallery for quite some time, wasn't it? Is she a relative of yours, Tracy?"

"I think that might have been my mother, and I was hoping you could either confirm or deny it. I have a picture here, and I was wondering if you would take a look at it."

Nora studied the picture for a long time. "I can't say for sure, but as I recall she looked a lot like you, what with that long blonde hair and all. I might be able to do better than that, though. I used to keep a guest book and asked each of my summer people to write a page or two in it before they left. What is your mother's name?"

"Laura Ratcliffe."

"Oh, that name does sound so familiar. Let me see if I can find that guest book. I haven't looked at it in years, but I think I know where it might be. I'll just be a minute."

Nora's minute seemed like an hour, but true to her word she came back clutching a yellowed journal-type book. She flipped through it and stopped at a page, reading to herself.

Please, Tracy thought. *Don't keep me in suspense. You have no idea how important this is to me.*

"Here it is right here… Laura Ratcliffe. She was here the summer of '82. She wrote two full pages. Kind words about how much she enjoyed staying here. Such a lovely young lady. I remember something else you might like to know, too. As I said before, we wrote letters back and forth for about a year. I recall now that she told me about expecting a child, a girl. Lost touch with her after that. Chalked it up to her being busy with a new baby. Was that you, by chance?"

"Yes, I was born in March of '83." As soon as the words were out of Tracy's mouth, the enormity of what she had just said hit her, and she felt weak and dizzy. Kate must have done the math in her head, too, and noticed Tracy's condition because she reached over and took her hand.

"Thank you, Nora," she said, realizing Tracy's inability to speak. "That answers Tracy's question about when her mother was in our village. I had told her about the portrait that looked so much like her, and she was just curious to know if it could have been her mother. And you've answered our question. We don't want to keep you any longer. Thank you for having us over at such short notice. And thank you for the tea."

"Of course. My summer people used to have tea with me, but since I quit renting the room, I have to take it by myself all too often. I'm pleased to have met you, Tracy, after all these years… and glad I was able to give you the information you needed. Please relay to your mother my fond memories of her and the summer she spent here in Wentworth Cove."

Tracy had recovered enough to say, "Thank you so much. I'll be sure to tell my mother I met you."

"Yes, do that. I would love to see her again if she is ever up this way. Oh, what a lovely young woman she was," Nora said as she let them out the door.

Their departure from Nora's house was quick but almost not quick enough for Tracy. As soon as they were in the safety of Kate's Jeep, she dissolved into a sea of tears. Kate backed out of the driveway quickly and in a couple of minutes pulled up in front of Grayson Cottage.

They sat there for a few minutes, neither one of them saying anything. Words were not necessary. They both knew.

"Tracy," Kate said after a while, "you can either come home with me, or I can come in with you, or you can be by yourself right now. I'll do whatever you want me to do. I just want you to know I'm here for you—whatever you need, whenever you need it."

"Thank you," Tracy managed through her tears. "I appreciate your taking me to Nora's, but I think I'd like to be by myself right now, though."

She closed the door behind her, alone with her thoughts, thinking maybe she should have let Kate stay. Thinking maybe she couldn't handle this new revelation by herself. But she realized this was something she had to do on her own. No one else could do for her now what she had to do for herself—accept the fact that John Strong was her father, not Kenneth Ratcliffe. Not the man who had taught her how to read, how to ride a bicycle, how to live life to the fullest. She remembered the first time her dad had taken her wading in the ocean—she couldn't have been more than three or four—and she was scared of the fish. She thought they would bite, but he said, "Don't be afraid, Tracy. They're just trying to give you kisses," and she was no longer afraid.

Dad, please come back. I need you now more than ever before. I need you to tell me everything's going to be all right. I need to put my arms around you and tell you that no matter what has happened in the past and no matter what happens in the future, you will always be my daddy.

Then, slowly creeping into her consciousness was a thought even more repugnant than her finding out the truth for herself. Her father must have known. He had to have known. He *had* to. If what her mother had told her was true and he was in England all of June and July while she was here, she was pregnant when he returned. Tracy was born in March; he could do the math, too. For some unknown reason, that realization hurt her even more than the first, and she collapsed on the bed and cried herself into exhaustion and eventually fitful sleep.

When she awoke at three, her stomach reminded her that she'd had no lunch. Nothing sounded good, but she forced herself to make a sandwich and take a few bites.

How could she ever speak to her mother again? How could things ever be the same between them? Would they forever be stuck in that tenuous relationship of her teen years when they barely tolerated each other? Should she tell her mother what she had found out today? Laura had always been able to read Tracy like a book; she would know something was wrong. It would all come out eventually, but Tracy needed time—time and a miracle—to enable her to deal with this.

After a few hours, a knock at the door interrupted her thoughts. She looked at her watch. Five-thirty. Who could that be, she wondered. She didn't know many people in Wentworth Cove. Figuring it was probably Kate coming to check on her, she opened the door without thinking about how she looked after an afternoon of sobbing, wiping her eyes, and blowing her nose.

Standing on the front porch, looking more handsome than ever, was Nathan. And for the second time that day, she was unable to speak.

Nathan broke the silence. "I was going for a sunset walk along the shore and wondered if you would like to go, too. I remember you walked by yourself one time but thought you might not mind some company today." If he noticed anything was wrong, he didn't show it.

"Did Kate send you over to check on me?" Tracy blurted out, more from embarrassment than anything else. As soon as the words were out, she wished more than anything that she could take them back.

"Of course not. Don't you think that at thirty I can make these decisions for myself?" Fortunately, he was smiling when he said it.

"I'm sorry. I didn't mean that." *Get a grip, Tracy.* "Have you talked to your mother today?"

"No. Why?"

"Nothing. I just had a difficult day and thought maybe she had sent you over to be an angel of mercy."

"I really came because I enjoy your company… and since I failed to ask for your phone number last night, but if this is not a good time…"

"No. I'd like to walk on the beach. If you wouldn't mind waiting a couple of minutes."

"Take your time. I'll just sit here and read this Welty novel and find out more about the South. Are you reading it?"

"No, I've read it. I just bought it to finish out my Eudora Welty collection."

Tracy had to hand it to him. He knew how to get her mind off her troubles. She was excited to have someone to talk to who knew Eudora Welty wrote about the South. His looking absolutely fabulous in faded jeans and a navy sweatshirt didn't hurt matters any either.

There was not much she could do to her hair but pull it back into a ponytail, but she remembered that the first day she'd seen Nathan her hair had been in a ponytail and she hadn't had on any makeup. Today she needed a little touch-up to cover the redness under her eyes, which he had already seen but was too much of a gentleman to mention. Tracy was presentable in about five minutes and didn't want to keep him waiting any longer.

"I'm ready. Sorry to keep you waiting."

"No problem. That was pretty fast really."

He had brought his car, so they drove about half a mile before they parked, got out, and started walking. In her haste, Tracy had forgotten to put on good walking shoes in case they had to climb over rocks, but it was too late to do anything about that now.

They walked for a while before either one of them spoke. Then Nathan said, "You know, the house you're staying in used to belong to Mrs. Grayson. She was my senior English teacher in high school."

"Yours, too? She must have taught everyone in Wentworth Cove at one time or another."

"At the time of her retirement about five years ago, she'd been teaching for forty years. Many of her former students don't live here anymore. She always encouraged us to follow our dreams, to go out and make a difference in the world. I don't know anyone who could inspire people the way she did."

"My dad was like that. His students always came back to tell him what a difference he'd made in their lives." Her dad. He would always be her dad, and she would not quit telling everyone who would listen how proud she was of him.

"Where does your dad teach?" Nathan inquired.

"He passed away two weeks after I graduated from college, but he was a professor of English Literature at Harvard."

71

"That must have been very difficult for you. I lost my father, too, a few years ago. That's not something you ever get over completely, is it?"

"No, it isn't."

They followed the shoreline to the south farther than Tracy had ventured by herself, but she assumed Nathan knew where he was going and when to turn around. Usually she would have been more conversant, but today was not usual. She was emotionally drained and not really up to carrying the burden for thinking about something to talk about. Fortunately, Nathan didn't seem to mind just walking, and they settled into a mutually comfortable silence. The contentment she felt with him now was such a contrast to the way she felt when she'd run into him on the deck of the art gallery. Only time would tell for sure, but it was apparently a major misjudgment on her part, and she chided herself once again for her bad habit of jumping to conclusions.

Nathan broke the silence by asking, "What do you do when you're not walking along the Maine coast?"

"Do you mean in Wentworth Cove or in Boston?"

"Let's start with Boston."

"I'm a literary agent. I've been with the same agency since my graduation from Boston College. How about you? When you're not taking care of children at day camp. Maggie told me about that."

"It seems we both work with words. I write them and you read them. I'm a copywriter for a retail clothing and housewares catalog. And, of course, I'm writing 'the great American novel' in my spare time. I'm sure you've heard that before, haven't you?"

"A few times, but when you say it, for some reason I believe it. What catalog do you write for?"

"Moose Creek Outfitters. They have a location in Kennebunkport, but their main offices are north of here in Camden."

"No way! That's you? Your mother gave me one of the catalogs, but she never mentioned—"

"No, I don't imagine she would. I think she would like to see me with a 'real job.' She'd like for me to be married, living in a rose-covered cottage surrounded by a picket fence, with one child and another on the way. I don't think she likes the idea that Jess is going to be her only grandchild, and apparently David and Elizabeth aren't going to oblige her with any more grandchildren."

"Are you the only one who writes the copy for the catalog? It's amazingly descriptive and captivating."

"I'll take that as quite a compliment from someone who's a real, live literary agent. I've been writing solo for them for two years. Before that, I wrote copy for an ad agency in Kennebunk, but it didn't leave me enough time to pursue my dream. I didn't think Mrs. Grayson would approve." He smiled, and his dimple worked its magic on Tracy. She was surprised to feel herself blushing. "So I quit and haven't regretted it for a minute. David and Elizabeth were kind enough to let me make an apartment out of the part of the gallery they weren't using, and the rent is minimal. I know I'm fortunate to have so much time to write now."

"I'd like to read your manuscript sometime," Tracy said earnestly. She'd met people who tried to take advantage of knowing a literary agent but sensed that Nathan was not one of those.

"Why don't I just send you a copy when it's published? I don't want to take advantage of our friendship. Anyway, I don't think it's ready for public consumption. I'm still in the revising and editing phase."

"I'd really like to read it, Nathan."

"No, I don't think so. Let's not mix business with pleasure." And that was that. The conversation about his novel and her getting to read it was over. She was relieved in a way, though. There were people who would have taken advantage of the fact that she was a literary agent. It would have been so easy for him to say, "Sure. I'd love for you to read it. Thanks." But he didn't. And for that she was grateful.

By this time they had turned back north and were almost back to where Nathan's car was parked. Tracy didn't look forward to going back to the cottage, alone once again with her thoughts, but she couldn't talk to Nathan about that. Not yet. She didn't know him well enough. She'd always been a private person. Kate was the only one who would know for now, and Tracy trusted her not to say anything to anyone else.

Nathan walked her to the door, and she invited him in.

"I'd better not," he responded, "I have to drive up to Camden tomorrow to pick up some of the clothes I'll be writing about for the next edition of the catalog."

"Well, thanks for the walk. It was just what the doctor ordered tonight."

"Oh, hey. Would you like to ride up to Camden with me tomorrow? It takes about two hours, and I'll be leaving around nine. I'd enjoy the company if you're not busy with something else. Have you ever been to Camden?"

"Once, a very long time ago," Tracy paused, remembering the last time she and her mom and her dad had driven up the Maine coast. Did she really want to go there right now? And yet. It would be a chance to spend more time with Nathan, get to know him better. And it would take her mind off the summer of '82.

"Sure. I'd love to go."

"Great. I'll pick you up at nine then?"

"Yeah. I'll be ready."

Chapter Nine

She could understand her mother's desire to conceal an affair she had before Tracy was born, but she still thought Laura owed her the truth about who her father was. *Was she ever planning to tell me?* Tracy wondered. Laura had never been one to share her deepest feelings with her daughter; Tracy assumed she shared them with her husband, though. Now she thought maybe her mother had held everything inside and she was the only one who truly knew the person she really was. Laura's parents had both died in an automobile accident when Tracy was only five years old. Did they carry any secrets they knew about Laura to their graves with them? And most important of all, how much did her dad know about this? She couldn't bear the thought that he might have endured insufferable pain all these years.

If he had ever thought of Tracy as anything other than his own daughter, he never gave her any indication. No one could have been a more doting father, always making time for her. She could never remember a time when he hadn't put down the newspaper when she crawled into his lap, when he said "No, not now" if Tracy wanted to talk to him about a problem, or when he failed to stop what he was doing and read a story she had written. *Dad, I really need you now. I need you now more than I ever did when you were alive.*

She had managed to escape her thoughts somewhat when she was with Nathan and was looking forward to spending more time with him. She realized now that he had that same sense of approachability Kate had. Tracy wanted to be able to talk to him about her discovery but worried it was too early in their friendship to disclose something so intensely personal, so she determined to keep their time together on a more casual level.

True to his word, Nathan arrived at nine o'clock sharp Wednesday morning. He was dressed in khaki shorts and a light blue chambray shirt with the sleeves rolled up. When Tracy opened the door, she could smell him, a scent new to her, but it was totally Nathan. She didn't know what it was—she'd been alone with him before—but all of a sudden she felt that same tingle of excitement she used to feel when she would go out on one of the few dates she had in high school. Maybe it was the realization they would be spending hours instead of minutes together this time. Maybe it was the fact that every time she saw him he looked more appealing.

"Come in," Tracy said, opening the door and feeling his warmth as he brushed past her. "I'll be just a minute. You know where the kitchen is. I made a pot of coffee. Help yourself."

"That sounds good. Don't rush. I allowed a little extra time to show you around Camden. My appointment's not until one o'clock."

Tracy disappeared into the bedroom, partly to finish getting ready, partly to gather her composure. The more she was around Nathan, the more he affected her.

In a couple of minutes, she walked back into the kitchen where Nathan was sitting at the table slowly sipping his coffee, a pensive look on his face.

"I'm ready," Tracy announced.

"You might want to bring your camera if you have one," he advised. "I have a feeling you're going to see some things you might want to take back to Boston with you."

I think I'm looking at one now, she thought before she willed herself back to reality. "That's a great idea. I can't believe I haven't taken any pictures since I arrived. Let me get it." Tracy went into the bedroom, took her camera out of her suitcase, dropped it into her purse and walked back into the kitchen. "I think I'm really ready now."

The drive along Highway 1 was scenic as it threaded its way through Biddeford, Bath, Damariscotta and Rockland, and Tracy asked Nathan three or four times if he would mind stopping for a minute so she could capture an image, glad he'd reminded her to bring the camera.

They talked mostly about their childhoods—vacations they'd taken with their families, field trips they'd gone on with their schools, and family traditions that still meant a lot to them, such as watching license plates and counting how many different states they saw. Both of their families played word games, and they compared notes on those. They also discussed foods they liked, pets they'd had as children, and, of course, Tracy told him about Molly. There were periods of silence too, just like when they had walked along the beach, but the silences weren't long and seemed very natural to Tracy. After a short time, one of them would think of something else to say, and off they would be on another topic.

When they finally pulled in to Camden, Nathan asked Tracy what she was hungry for, and she chose seafood. It was time, she figured, to have another bowl of clam chowder.

They ate, mostly in that comfortable silence that had become commonplace to them, and when Tracy had taken the last spoonful of her soup, Nathan broke the silence.

"So I asked my mom if she knew why you would have thought she told me to check on you the other day."

"What did she say?"

"She said not to press you to talk about it if you didn't want to."

"That sounds just like Kate. She's so thoughtful and sensitive to other people's feelings."

"Yes, she is. Do you?"

"Do I what?"

"Want to talk about it?"

Tracy hadn't thought he would be so direct, and she guessed it was a combination of his directness, getting her mind back on the "John Strong" situation and the conflicting feelings she had about Nathan at that time, but her emotions overwhelmed her to the point that she could no longer control them. Tears flooded her eyes and she couldn't speak. And the warmth of Nathan's hand on her shoulder caused even more of her pent up emotions to come flowing out. All at once she felt herself enveloped in his arms where, she thought, it might be nice to stay forever.

"I'm sorry, Tracy," he whispered in her ear. "I didn't mean to bring up something that would make you cry. But if it makes you feel better, go ahead. It's probably not good to hold it in."

She buried her face in his chest and his arms tightened around her. He held her as she sobbed and after a couple of minutes took her hand and led her out of the restaurant, down the street, and over to a bench overlooking the harbor. They sat without speaking for a few minutes, his hand still tenderly encircling hers.

"Tracy, I would never try to force you to talk about it if you didn't want to, but I have a feeling that if something is bothering you this much, you don't need to keep it cooped up inside. Does my mother know about it?"

"Yes."

"Then if you want to talk only to her about it, that's okay, but if you ever want someone else to talk to, I'll be here. I care about you and don't like to think that anything or anyone has hurt you this much."

"Not right now, but maybe later, Nathan. And thanks for being so understanding. I see it runs in the Norsworthy family. I must look awful."

"You could never look awful. Even with tear-stained cheeks and a red nose, you still look great to me."

They sat like that in silence, her hand in his, for a few more minutes before he said, "Are you ready to see more of Camden now? I have to pick up some clothes from the office, but that won't take but a couple of minutes."

"Yeah. I'd like that."

After Nathan had put the clothes in his car, he and Tracy drove downtown again and strolled along the harbor, Tracy taking pictures of boats, stores, people and flowers along the way.

They got back in the car and explored Camden's beautiful neighborhoods full of whitewashed houses and flower-laden front yards. They drove to Mount Battie, climbed to the top, and Tracy took pictures of the boats in the harbor.

"Ready to head back to Wentworth Cove, Tracy?"

"Yes, but it's been a wonderful day. Thank you so much for letting me tag along with you on your business trip."

"I enjoyed it, too. I travel up here about once a month, but it's been like seeing it for the first time looking at it today through your eyes. You take so much pleasure in the beauty of the scenery. Sometimes I think I take it for granted and tend to forget that I get to drive one of the most beautiful roads in the United States to go to work."

"When you're tempted to take it for granted again, just try to visualize my forty-five minute long commute into downtown Boston by commuter train every day."

"You take the train? How bad could it be? Just sit back, relax, and let someone else do the driving." Nathan obviously hadn't worked in a big city and had to deal with commuting.

"Well. It's like this," Tracy started, visualizing the train she took to Smithson Literary Agency five days a week. "The train is always packed, and the stops are all outside, so not fun in the winter and not fun in the summer when it's extremely hot. The line I take, the B line, has so many stops, three of which are at Boston College, and at night it's awful because it's full of rowdy, drunk college students. People are always trying to get on without paying, too, and the B trains sometimes collide with cars or cyclists. Now," she paused for effect and smiled, "does that answer your 'How bad could it be?' question?"

"It does. It does, but if I think about that, I'll just start feeling sorry for you, and then I won't enjoy anything," Nathan said and they both laughed.

They didn't talk as much on the way back to Wentworth Cove. Nathan turned on the radio and found a station they both liked, one that played music that had been popular while they were in high school, and they had fun reminiscing. Sometimes when a song would start playing, one of them would recall special memories it evoked. They were both careful, however, not to mention people they'd dated. Tracy hadn't dated much in high school, and she had the feeling he hadn't either—mostly, she guessed, because Maggie had talked about how shy he was.

When they pulled up in front of the cottage, Nathan got out of the car and came around to open the door. He held her hand as they walked to the front door and once there, he took both of hers in his. "Going to pick up clothes in Camden has never been so much fun. I'm glad you went with me."

"So am I," Tracy admitted, an unexpected warmth beginning to flow through her body.

"And remember, if you ever want someone to talk to, I would consider it an honor to be chosen. Of course, if you like my mother better…"

"It's not that. It's just that—"

"I was kidding. I totally understand. And I'll have to agree. My mom is easy to talk to."

"I was going to say it's just that she knows the situation, and I don't have to explain anything to her."

"That's okay, but I do want to see you again soon—if that's all right with you."

"It's quite all right with me. I pretty much have an open calendar for the next couple of weeks."

"The next couple of weeks? You're leaving in two weeks? I just assumed you were staying longer. Most people who come here stay the whole summer."

"I'd like to, but I get only four weeks of vacation." *If you only knew how much I would like to.*

"I guess it's been too long since I had a real job. I forget about things like that."

"I wish I could forget, but unfortunately, when I get back to Boston, I'll probably have ten manuscripts on my desk waiting for me and another forty or fifty in my inbox."

"Well, I suppose if duty calls, you have to answer."

"I guess so…since I've grown accustomed to eating and sleeping in a warm apartment."

"Um, guess I'd better get started on the copy for these clothes. I'll see you again soon, though." He turned and as Tracy watched him walk back to his car, she was alone once again with her thoughts—thoughts of more than just John now. Thoughts of Nathan and how much she enjoyed being with him, of where this relationship could go, of whether she should open up her heart to him with only two more weeks left in Wentworth Cove, Maine.

Chapter Ten

More than ever Tracy needed someone to talk to, but she wasn't prepared to call her mother yet and didn't think it fair to talk to Kate about Nathan. There wasn't really anyone else she would share her feelings with except Gina, her college roommate and best friend. They'd lived together for two years in the dorm and shared an apartment close to campus for the last two years of college. Although Gina was now married to Todd Lundsford and living in Vermont, they still talked and texted at least once or twice a week. Tracy had been maid-of-honor in her wedding and was godmother to her three-year-old son, Hunter. Seeing her face to face was preferable to talking on the phone, but since she lived a good four hours away, Tracy took her phone out of her bag and dialed Gina's number.

"Hello," said a sweet voice on the other end of the line. She still had a little girl quality about her that Tracy loved. She assumed Gina would always be a child at heart. Todd had swept her off her feet their senior year in college. They married three months after graduation, so she had never really had to take care of herself, and since Todd was more than able to support her financially, she had never worked. She had someone to clean her house once a week and she didn't cook, but Todd and Gina were happy with their lifestyle and Tracy was happy for them.

"Hi, Gina. How are you?"

"Wonderful. I'm so glad it's you, Tracy. I wanted to know how your vacation is going, but I didn't know how to get in touch with you. I tried your cell a couple of times. Are you not carrying it around with you? Did you see my text?" That must have seemed very strange to Gina, given Tracy's past addiction to her phone.

"No. I came here for a vacation, and I'm doing it right. I vacated the phone, too. How are things in Woodstock? How are Todd and Hunter?"

"Everyone's great. Are you having a good time?"

"Yes and no. In fact, that's why I called. Do you have time to talk right now?"

"Of course. Todd's working late tonight, and Hunter's playing with the little boy next door. I was just getting ready to settle down with a good book, but from the sound of your voice, what you're about to tell me is much more interesting. Are you okay?" Tracy had to give it to Gina. She was extremely perceptive and could always read her.

"I guess that good news-bad news cliché fits here. Which do you want first?"

"Ordinarily I would say let's start with the bad and get it over with, but I'm too curious about the good. Have you met someone?"

"You know me too well."

"I knew it had to happen sometime. Tell me everything—all the juicy details."

"There aren't any juicy details. He hasn't even kissed me, but I can't describe the way I feel when I'm with him. If I had to sum it up in one word, it would have to be comfortable, but I can't do that because it's more than that. I feel like a giddy schoolgirl, too."

"What's his name? How'd you meet him? Does he live there? What does he look like?"

"Whoa! Slow down, girl. His name's Nathan Norsworthy. I met his family first. He's lived in Wentworth Cove all his life. He's gorgeous—tall, dark brown hair and the most amazing light gray-green eyes you could imagine."

"Wow! I don't even want to know the bad news after all that. Is it about him?"

"No, but I'm not sure where this is going. After all, I'm leaving in two weeks."

"Don't start doing that again, Tracy."

"Doing what?"

"Borrowing trouble. You always do that. How many times have I had to fuss at you about worrying about things that weren't worth worrying about? Just enjoy your time there with him and see what happens. I'm warning you, Tracy. Don't mess this up, or I'll be really mad at you."

"I guess I just wanted to hear you say for reassurance that I wasn't thinking with something other than my head."

"That's your problem. You think with your head too much. What else is going on over there?"

There was no use beating around the bush with Gina. She would get it out of Tracy sooner or later, so she blurted it out, "I found out my mother had an affair with another man the summer she was up here and—" Tracy's voice broke.

"What? Tracy, I can't believe that. But go on. What else?"

"My dad… isn't my real father." The hot tears came again and Gina and Tracy sat in silence for a minute.

"I don't believe that, Tracy. You and your dad were like two peas in a pod, alike in every way. Do you know that for a fact?"

"Yes. I found out my mother was here the summer, June and July anyway, before I was born in March. And my dad was away studying at Oxford for those two months. You do the math. I've tried and I've tried, and I can't make two plus two equal five."

"Oh, Trace. Do you need me to come up? I could bring Hunter and drive up there tomorrow and stay with you a couple of days."

"No. I'm all right. There's someone here who was with me when I found out, Nathan's mother, in fact. I met her the first day I was here, and she's been great. She lives two doors down from where I'm staying."

"Does Nathan know?"

"No. I haven't told him yet; although, we drove up to Camden today, and he knew something was wrong. He was wonderful."

"Do you know who he is—your real father, I mean? Oh, Tracy. Kenneth Ratcliffe was your *real* father. I mean your biological father."

"Yes. I've met him, but he doesn't have any idea that I know anything. I don't even know if *he* knows. Oh, Gina, I don't know what to do. I've always been on top of everything, but I feel as though the earth is crumbling under my feet. I can't even make any decisions for myself anymore."

"Then let me make them for you while you're in this state of mind. You have to tell him you know. It isn't fair to him not to. Does your mother know you know?"

"She doesn't have a clue. Actually, I haven't talked to her since I found out a couple of days ago."

"Are you going to tell her?"

"Not yet. I have some decisions to make first. Gina, the battery is about to run down on my phone, so I'd better sign off, but I'll call you again soon."

"Please do. Don't leave me in suspense. And take my advice. Honesty really is the best policy, you know. I know you hate clichés, but it fits here."

"You're probably right, but it won't be easy."

"I know. But it will be worth it."

"I'll call you tomorrow. Thanks for everything."

"I'm glad you called, Trace. Love you."

Hanging up the phone, Tracy thought about Gina's advice. She wanted to believe Gina was right about Nathan, that she should quit worrying and let her heart take over for a change. No one had ever made her feel the way Nathan made her feel, and she'd known him only a few days.

Right now, though, she was thinking about John. She planned to walk down to Kate's house in the morning and try to find out more about him. She had some difficult decisions to make and needed more information before she could make them.

Knocking lightly on her neighbor's door the next morning, she called out, "Kate, it's Tracy."

"Come in. I was just thinking about you, but I couldn't decide whether or not to come over since you needed to be alone the other day."

"I haven't really been alone much since I saw you last, thanks to Nathan. And I am very grateful to him. Although he doesn't know the whole situation, he could tell I was upset and has been very kind and understanding. He came over Tuesday night and we walked on the beach. Then yesterday I rode up to Camden with him when he went to pick up some clothes from Moose Creek Outfitters. Why didn't you tell me he wrote the copy for the catalog you gave me? He's so talented and creative."

"So Nathan's been taking care of you all this time, has he? I'm glad to hear that. But I didn't tell him anything; I haven't talked to anyone. I guess he just decided to come over on his own, which is not really like him. He's usually rather reserved, but I could tell Monday night that he was interested."

Feeling a little guilty talking about Nathan with his mother, Tracy thought about trying to change the subject, but she was too intrigued and wanted to know more about him, so she decided to keep the conversation going.

"When I first met him, I thought he never said more than one or two words at a time, but now I realize that he thinks before he speaks, and unless he has something he feels is worth saying, he just doesn't say anything at all."

"He's very private in many ways and definitely not a man of many words, until he feels that he knows someone pretty well, anyway. Spoken words, I should say. Written words—now that's a different matter altogether. He's always had a talent for writing. But that might just be a mother talking."

There was so much Tracy wanted to know about Nathan, and she sensed that Kate didn't mind talking about him, so she asked about his job as a catalog copywriter.

"I was pretty upset when he gave up a lucrative position with the ad agency in Kennebunkport, but I've come to think it was the right decision for him. He's never been happier. Money and material possessions are not important to him. He's happy simply taking care of his kids and writing his book. Did I tell you he volunteers at the YMCA day camps each summer?" Kate was obviously proud of Nathan, but from a couple of things he had said, Tracy had the feeling he wasn't so sure of that.

"Maggie told me about that when I saw him in the Fourth of July parade surrounded by all those kids. He looked as though he belonged there."

"There was a time when I thought he and Maggie might be an item. She's a nice girl, but I guess what they have is just a friendship. It's hard to know with Nathan.

David was much more open. We always knew everything about him because he talked so much. He called us the night he met Elizabeth at college and said that he had met the girl he was going to marry, and then he called about once a week to update us on how the relationship was going. Nathan would never do that; in fact, I doubt he'll even mention to me that he has seen you."

At that moment the phone rang in the other room, and Kate went to answer it. She was gone for about five minutes. When she walked back into the living room, Tracy could tell she was trying to suppress a grin. "Well, I've been wrong before, and I'll be wrong again, but I guess I don't know my son as well as I thought I did. That was Nathan telling me he had seen you twice this week and asking me if I knew whether or not you liked sailing. He thought he remembered hearing you mention it the other day. It seems he has plans. I didn't tell him you were here."

"Good," Tracy said, blushing. Why did she feel like a conspirator? Would he mind if he knew she was at his mother's house talking about him?

"Do you like to sail? I took the liberty of saying that I was pretty sure you did. You don't get seasick or anything like that, do you?"

"No. I love sailing. It's one of the things my dad and I did together." The mention of her dad reminded Tracy why she'd come over to Kate's house.

"Be expecting an invitation soon then."

"Kate, I was wondering if you could tell me any more about John. I'm in a quandary about what to do, and of course I can't talk to my mom about it. I called a friend, and she thought I should tell them both that I know."

"If you're asking my advice, Tracy, I've always hated family secrets. They put a strain on all the relationships involved." Tracy knew Kate was right, but that didn't make what she was facing any easier. She was beginning to feel sick again, the way she felt every time she talked or even thought about the situation.

"My mom will know something's wrong as soon as she sees me anyway. I know I have to do something. I just don't know how to go about it."

"How would you like to get to know John better first, in a non-threatening setting? I could invite you both over here, or we could drive up to Kennebunk and go to lunch with him. I do that occasionally anyway, so he wouldn't think it strange."

"That's a good idea. Do you think we could do that soon? I only have two more weeks to get everything resolved. I can't go home not knowing for sure."

"Of course. I'll call and see when he's free."

"Thank you. I don't know what I'd do without you. I had no idea when I first drove down Old Sea Pines Road and pulled up in front of Grayson Cottage that my life would change so much in just two weeks. I appreciate your friendship."

"And I yours. You add a lot to our sleepy, little village. I wish your stay wasn't so short… and I have a feeling I'm not the only one who feels that way."

Tracy felt the blood rushing to her cheeks again. Bidding Kate goodbye, she walked out into the sunlight of a glorious summer day in Wentworth Cove, Maine. The rest of the day loomed before her, and she longed to occupy her thoughts with something other than John Strong. She was sure her mother was wondering why she hadn't called again. Maybe she should get in touch with her so she wouldn't worry.

Walking back to the cottage, she breathed in the salt sea air and felt a new exhilaration, a new inner strength. She had learned to be strong from her father, and she didn't think he would want her to give in to this situation. She would see it through to the end.

Chapter Eleven

True to her word, Kate came over the next morning with a lunch invitation. They would meet John at eleven thirty in Kennebunk, and Tracy could feel free to take the conversation wherever she wanted it to go. That was a scary thought. She didn't know where she wanted it to go.

The drive into town was quiet, and Tracy was alone with her thoughts as her eyes took in the sights of a place she was growing rather fond of. A picturesque fishing village dotted with white clapboard houses and church steeples.

As Kate's Jeep pulled up in front of their designated meeting place, Spinnaker's, a wave of queasiness reminded Tracy that this was not just a social meeting with one of Kate's lifelong friends. This was possibly her first in-depth conversation with her biological father. Her cotton-dry mouth and the lump in her throat wouldn't let her forget the real reason they were there.

"Kate, I don't think I can do this. All of a sudden I feel weak and incapable."

"You really don't have any choice, do you? You can't spend the rest of your life wondering, wondering what kind of person he is and not giving him a chance. I'll be right here with you. I'll speak up if the conversation starts to lag, and if you want to keep it light and impersonal, that's fine. That's John's silver Volvo over there. He's waiting for us inside. Are you ready?"

Ready for what? Ready to toss life as she knew it, as she had always known it, into the ocean? Ready to accept this man she didn't even know as her father? Ready to acknowledge that her mother was unfaithful to the man who had always been a real father to her? Even if she was ready for all these things, she felt sure she was not ready to forgive her mother for what she had done to both of them.

John rose as they neared the table, kissed Kate on the cheek and took both of Tracy's hands, sweaty palms and all, in his. "This is such a treat. It's not every day that I have lunch with two beautiful women. I'm so glad you called, Kate, and glad you brought Tracy with you."

Apparently trying to make it seem natural and uncontrived, Kate responded as they sat down, "It's been a long time since we've done this, hasn't it? I guess we all get so involved in our day-to-day activities that we forget to keep our friendships in repair. David's home from his Bar Harbor buying trip, so they don't really need me as much at the gallery. Besides, I'm trying to keep Tracy from getting bored in our little village so she won't be in such a hurry to get back to the bright lights of the big city."

"That's right. You're from Boston, aren't you?" Tracy was not surprised that John remembered this bit of information.

She took a deep breath to relax, hoping her voice would not betray her. "Yes, but I haven't had any time to get bored. I haven't even read those books I checked out the other day. Kate and her family have been gracious enough to see that I am entertained most of the time."

"It seems that my baby boy has been sacrificing and showing Tracy the sights, too. He drove her up to Camden the other day when he went on one of his clothing runs."

"Ah, Nathan. I'm not surprised. I always knew that boy had good taste. He hasn't let you read that book he's writing, has he?"

"No, he hasn't. But I did ask."

"I have faith in that boy. He told me once that he doesn't plan to let anyone read it until it's published—and he qualified that with 'if'—but I think we'll all get a chance to read it one of these days. Have you seen any of his work in the Moose Creek Outfitters catalog?"

"Yes, and I was impressed by the copy even before I knew who wrote it. He does have talent."

"That's not just an offhand remark by an untrained eye, John," Kate inserted. "Tracy is a literary agent with an agency in Boston."

"Is that so? Which one?"

"Smithson Literary."

"A good, solid company. I mentor some aspiring writers, so I'm familiar with most of the large agencies. How long have you been with them, Tracy?"

"Since my graduation from Boston College about ten years ago. I started as an assistant and was able to work my way up pretty quickly."

Their food arrived, and they ate for a few minutes in silence. Fortunately, Tracy had ordered clam chowder again, her comfort food. It was outstanding and superseded Down East Diner as number one in her rankings. Kate and John had both ordered the shrimp scampi.

John broke the silence with a question she'd been halfway expecting, and the butterflies fluttered again in her stomach. "Tracy, didn't you say, the first time we met, that your mother is a librarian?"

She braced herself once more to answer his question. "Yes. She's with the Boston Public Library system and manages the Brighton branch."

"What about your father? What does he do?"

She hadn't expected that one, and it hit her pretty hard. In what must have seemed like a futile attempt to John and Kate to gain her composure, she stammered, "He… He passed away two weeks after I graduated from college."

"I'm so sorry to hear that."

In an obvious—or so it seemed to Tracy anyway— attempt to divert John's attention to another topic, Kate inserted, "John, do you remember that time we drove down to Ogunquit and went to see *Death of a Salesman* at the Ogunquit Playhouse? I was thinking Tracy might like to do that sometime. But, of course, I don't even know if she enjoys plays. Do you?"

"As a matter of fact, I do. That sounds like a fun evening. How far is Ogunquit? I think I remember driving through a town by that name on my way to Wentworth Cove."

"It's about fifteen miles from Kennebunk. I'll arrange something then," Kate said, "and if you don't mind, Tracy, I think I'll see if David and Elizabeth would like to join us. Elizabeth loves the theater."

"I'd like that. I want to get to know them better."

Their check came, and although they both tried, John wouldn't let them pay. They made some more small talk in the parking lot, and then John got in his silver Volvo and drove away. Had the meeting accomplished anything? Tracy didn't know, but she did know that she couldn't feel any hatred for him. He was a gentleman. He exuded class. He wasn't married thirty-two years ago, but her mother was. Did he know? That didn't matter to her as much as the fact that Laura knew. That's what kept coming back to haunt her. That and wondering whether her father ever suspected anything.

Chapter Twelve

After returning to the cottage, Tracy's conflicted emotions made her restless, and she set out for the ocean, hoping the regularity and reliability of the waves could soothe her soul as they had so many times in the past. The sun had burned away the morning haze, and the day had turned golden. She marveled at the difference in sounds in Wentworth Cove and the ones she was used to in Boston. No car horns sending impatient messages to other drivers. No sirens from emergency vehicles. No cell phones ringing or voices offering conversations that should be kept private. Only the occasional sound of a songbird in a willow tree breaking the silence. Or in the distance, some children laughing and playing tag.

She passed couples as she ambled down the coastline and once again thought about how it would be to have someone to share this time with—a shoulder to cry on, a sympathetic ear to listen as she tried to sort out her feelings. For a few seconds she allowed herself to think about Nathan as that "someone." He would be sympathetic—that she knew—but was she ready to open herself up to him in that way? After all, she'd known him only a couple of weeks.

Lost in thought, she didn't hear the footsteps coming up behind her. A gentle tap on her shoulder as he said her name quietly. "Tracy. I thought I might find you here."

"Nathan, I didn't expect—"

"I know, but since there's no phone in the cottage and you said you were keeping your cell phone turned off—and you weren't home when I went by, I took a chance. If this isn't a good time, though…"

"No. It's a great time. I just needed one of my therapeutic ocean walks."

"Do you mind if I join you or would you rather walk alone?"

Are you kidding? If you only knew how much I don't mind. "Of course not. I'd like the company. Sometimes I enjoy being alone out here, but this is not one of those times." She hoped that sounded casual enough and didn't give away her true feelings.

They walked without saying anything for a minute or two before Nathan broke the silence. "I'm sure you thought I was rude the first time we met—in the art gallery. Didn't you? As I recall, I wasn't very friendly when you tried to talk to me. Sometimes I don't know what gets into me when I'm writing. It's like I don't really sense anything but the words that are flowing through me. That's the only way I know to describe it—they just well up in my head, travel through my arms and hands, and come out my fingertips. Most of the time I don't even know I have them inside me. But enough of that. What I really wanted to say is I'm sorry if I came across as unfriendly."

Nathan was being honest, and Tracy felt she should, too. "I'll have to admit I was surprised on the Fourth when I got to know you a little better. I could tell I had misjudged you. And now that we've spent more time together, I think I'm beginning to know the real Nathan."

"I'd like to get to know the real Tracy. Tell me all about you. I know you don't like to cook, but what do you like to do? What kind of music do you like? What do you like to read? Tell me about your family."

"Whoa! Slow down. All of that could take a while."

"Well, as you've probably noticed, my time is my own to do with as I please as long as I manage to eat and keep a roof over my head. And right now what I want to do with it is find out more about you, so you have no excuse not to talk. I have all the time in the world."

Where did Tracy want this to go? Ordinarily, she would put on the brakes before something got started. After all, she had only two weeks left in Wentworth Cove. Why let it go any further? But she could hear Gina saying, "Don't mess this one up, Tracy," so she decided to jump in with both feet.

"Where should I start? And if I reveal my soul to you, you have to promise to reciprocate. Deal?"

"Deal. Start with the easy stuff, music and literature. You must like to read or else you wouldn't have become a literary agent, and I remember seeing some books in the living room of the cottage. Let's see…*The Ponder Heart* by Eudora Welty. Am I wrong? Is she your favorite author?"

"You're not wrong. I bought that book to finish out my Welty collection. I can't say I have a favorite, but she's one of many. I like Theodore Dreiser, Flannery O'Connor, T.S. Eliot, Amy Tan…How far do you want me to go? What about you? Do you have a favorite?"

"In high school I read Homer, Salinger, Fitzgerald, Orwell. Then in college I got on a Roald Dahl kick. Mrs. Grayson made sure we read a wide variety of authors. What about music? Any special era?"

"Eighties and nineties, I guess. That's what we grew up with, isn't it?"

"Anyone in particular?"

"Billy Joel, George Michael, James Taylor…My dad and I saw him in concert on Martha's Vineyard one time, and I was sold. I like just about everything he sings, especially the ones he writes himself."

"I remember you said your dad died right after you graduated from college, but what about your mother? Does she live in Boston? Any brothers or sisters?"

"My mom does live in Boston. She's a librarian. No brothers or sisters. Just a very spoiled Yorkshire terrier that my mom treats like another child. Her name is Molly. What about you? Have I met your whole family?"

"That's it except for some aunts, uncles and cousins. And, of course, my grandparents on my dad's side. They live in Bangor. I see them two or three times a year. My mom wanted us to stay close to them, especially after my dad died."

By this time they had come to some rocks and ledges, and Nathan took Tracy's hand to help her over them. The sensation of his touch and the tenderness in his eyes gave her a feeling of both warmth and excitement at the same time. He didn't let go once they were over the rock, and she was glad. They were becoming more comfortable with each other, and it was one of those moments that if she could have suspended time and made it last forever, she would have.

Nathan had released something in her that had been locked up for a long time. He possessed what she'd been looking for in a man—intelligence, looks, and charm—but more than that even. He had an irresistible magnetism. She'd heard it referred to as chemistry, but until that moment she had never experienced it for herself. Craig certainly hadn't stirred these feelings in her.

They walked along silently for a while, their hands readjusting and their fingers becoming intertwined, much as their souls were becoming. Suddenly, Nathan stopped and turning to face Tracy ever so slowly and softly, put his hand on the back of her head and gently drew her to him as his face reached down to hers. It happened so instinctively, so effortlessly, the way his lips met hers, tenderly, with not even the slightest hint of force. A whisper of a kiss, but it traveled all the way through her body, and she let him teach her a new song. A song she had never sung before.

"Tracy," Nathan whispered almost breathlessly, "I've been wanting to do that since I was at your house that night after the fireworks. I came close in Camden, but it didn't seem like the right time, and I want everything to be right with us."

He'd given her no reason to think he'd been considering anything of the sort, but it was as if a wall had fallen down from between them and there was no turning back.

"I didn't know you felt that way, but I can't honestly say I mind," Tracy murmured as she kissed him back.

There was a time when she would have run. But not now. Not from Nathan. There was no fear factor with him. She had no intention of "messing it up" as Gina would have put it. In the back of her mind there was always that thought that she had less than two weeks in Wentworth Cove, and what would happen when she had to go back to Boston. But for some reason, even that didn't worry her. This felt too right not to work out, and for once Tracy was going to relax and not try to do all the planning. Two weeks away from the office had been good for her in that regard. She no longer felt the need to be in control.

They walked back to Nathan's car, hand in hand. By the time they got there, they'd planned a dinner at the cottage and a Saturday of sailing. On the way to Carson's Market, Tracy mentally prepared a list for the only meal she felt totally competent making, lasagna and salad. Gina had once told her that all men like lasagna, so she felt safe there.

As they walked up and down the aisles at Carson's Market, Tracy made a mental note to call Gina soon. Gina would be so proud of her. It was also time to call her mother again, but she didn't think she was ready for that. Maybe in another day or two. She was sure Laura was wondering why she hadn't called again.

"Nathan, Tracy!" Annie Culwell—of all the people to run into. Although Tracy was perfectly comfortable with their relationship, she wasn't sure she was ready for the rest of the world to know about it.

Fortunately, Nathan didn't seem flustered. "Hi, Annie. What are you doing here?" he asked.

"It's my turn to cook tonight, and I don't usually like the options we have at our house, so I thought I'd look for something a little different. What do you suggest, Nathan?" *Nathan? Just Nathan? Not Nathan and Tracy? I'm here, too, you know, Annie.*

"Well, Tracy's making lasagna. Why don't you try that? I'm sure she'd be glad to give you her recipe, wouldn't you?"

"Sure. Hi, Annie. How's Maggie?"

"Maggie's fine. I didn't know you two knew each other." Did Tracy see darts in her eyes? "Except that time we all got together on the Fourth, I mean."

"We didn't really know each other then, but we do now," Nathan replied as he smiled at Tracy.

Annie didn't seem to like that answer. "I have to go now." She turned abruptly and called back over her shoulder, "Don't think I have time to get your recipe tonight, Tracy. Some other time, maybe," and she was gone. Just like that. She obviously didn't like what she had seen, and Tracy wondered what she would tell Maggie, if anything, about them. Maggie had said if anything were going to happen between her and Nathan, it would have happened by now, but apparently Annie didn't think that was necessarily the case. She was obviously still holding out hope. If Tracy hadn't been sure of it before, she was now.

Nathan didn't seem to have noticed anything unusual about Annie's abrupt exit. Tracy guessed he was relatively innocent as far as petty women were concerned. He didn't have any in his family, that was for sure. Jessica, who was only one year younger than Annie, was as opposite her in personality as she could possibly be, and Tracy knew that Nathan adored his niece. He probably thought all girls were as sweet and innocent as she was.

Tracy studied Nathan's profile as they drove back to the cottage. She had been on a roller coaster of emotions with the revelation about John Strong and her mother, but right now, as Robert Browning once wrote about moments like this, all was right with the world.

Chapter Thirteen

Dinner was a success. Tracy had proved to Nathan that she could do more than just read and critique manuscripts. She wasn't entirely helpless in the kitchen, and his compliments proved it.

Afterward, they sat in the backyard and watched as the sun's rays got lower and the shadows grew longer.

Out of the blue, Nathan asked, "What's your favorite Welty novel?" She didn't mind. She was just glad to be talking with someone who would actually recognize the title when she said it.

"*The Optimist's Daughter*. Why?"

"Just wondering. I want to know everything there is to know about you. Favorite Billy Joel song?"

"'Piano Man.'" Not wanting him to do all the discovering, she countered, "Two can play this game. Favorite Dickens novel?"

"Easy. *Tale of Two Cities*. Favorite T.S. Eliot poem?"

"'Love Song of J. Alfred Prufrock.' Favorite Orwell novel?"

"1984."

As they watched the last reds of the western sky give way to deep purples, and fireflies began to flicker around them, Nathan reached for Tracy's hand and pulled her up out of the chair. She stood silently before him, the lingering sensation of his touch staying with her. He kissed her once softly, then once again more ardently, and as she gave way to his embrace, she could almost hear the pounding of her heart against his chest.

"I have to go, Tracy," he said abruptly.

"No, you don't. It's not that late."

"Oh, yes, I do…I really do. Besides, you know that same sun we just witnessed sliding down that western slope a while ago? We need to be there when it peeks above the eastern horizon in the morning. There's only one thing more glorious than a sunset in Wentworth Cove, and that's a sunrise, especially with the wind on your face as you watch the shore getting smaller in the distance."

"No fair. You didn't warn me you were a morning person. I've just in the last two weeks trained myself to sleep past six, and now you want me to undo all that training just to go sailing with you?"

"Trust me. It'll be worth it," he replied, and Tracy had a feeling that was an enormous understatement.

The next morning she stumbled into the kitchen, poured a glass of orange juice and put on a pot of coffee. By the time the coffee brewed, Nathan had arrived, picnic basket in hand. "Don't bother with breakfast. I've slaved over a hot stove this morning preparing bagels with cream cheese and jelly, and I brought a thermos of hot tea. I need to pack some paper plates and napkins, though. Do you have some?" As he lounged against the counter, sipping his coffee, his stance casual and relaxed, her heart skipped a beat, and she marveled at how lucky she was.

"Sure. Look in the cabinet just behind you. I'll be ready in a minute."

Little did she know when she asked for a month off from Smithson Literary Agency that she would drive up to Wentworth Cove, Maine, and meet someone who would turn her life upside down. She hurried back into the bedroom to put the finishing touches on her makeup, thinking about the absurdity of what had been going on in her life since she'd arrived in that sleepy little village.

This isn't the way it's supposed to work, she thought as she whisked the mascara wand over her eyelashes. *I'm not supposed to fall in love with someone who lives almost a hundred miles away from Boston. I live in Boston; I work in Boston; my life is in Boston.*

Love? Who said anything about love? Nathan certainly hasn't. Slow down, Tracy. You're getting ahead of yourself. Relax and enjoy this time with him. It's been a long time since you've been sailing. Just try to take it one step at a time. And remember what Gina said. Don't mess this up.

Tracy took a deep breath and walked back into the kitchen. "I'm ready."

Soon they were enjoying the pleasant whoosh of the water as it flowed along the hull of the boat. Nathan had rented a 25-foot sloop, and they found the wind easily. The sloping and moving deck beneath her feet caused so many memories to flood her mind. They were good memories, though. She recalled something her dad had once told her about sailing. "Tracy, there will always be problems in life, and sailing is not an escape from those problems. It's not an escape from life on land, but it can be a journey toward a better understanding of it." *Thanks, Dad.*

Nathan's promise of a glorious sunrise was not overstated. The orange ball inched its way above the horizon, and the morning sky was streaked with fingertips of purple and rose.

Nathan's voice brought Tracy back to reality. "What are you thinking about?"

"My dad. Sailing always makes me think of him. It's been ten years, and I still miss him, you know."

"I *do* know. But I think it's healthy. If you didn't, something would be wrong."

"On my sixteenth birthday, he gave me a copy of Anne Morrow Lindbergh's *Gift From the Sea*. I sat down and read it from cover to cover—twice. And I've reread it every year on my birthday for the last fifteen years."

"'One should lie empty, open, choiceless as a beach— waiting for a gift from the sea.'"

"You know it, too. Why am I not surprised?" *Could this day get any better?* Tracy wondered.

As dawn morphed into morning, Nathan and Tracy discovered the romance of slow cruising as they ate their bagels and sipped steaming cups of Earl Grey tea. Conversation never lagged. It seemed as though they had two lifetimes of catching up to do. When they weren't talking about childhood memories or their families, Nathan would throw in a few minutes of "Favorites."

"Favorite Dreiser novel?" he would ask.

"*An American Tragedy*," she would respond. "Favorite Phil Collins song?"

"'Against All Odds.' Favorite Neil Diamond song?"

"'Heartlight.'"

When Tracy got back to the cottage that afternoon, she knew she had to make a phone call but wasn't looking forward to it. Her mother had probably been wondering why she hadn't heard from her in over a week. The knot in her stomach reminded her why she had put off this call.

She braced herself and dialed Laura's number.

"Hello."

"Mom, it's me."

"Tracy. Thank goodness you called. I was beginning to worry about you. I hope this means you're too busy having a good time to think about us poor souls stuck back here in the concrete jungle."

"I'm fine. I guess I've just been staying kind of busy, though."

"I can usually read you, Trace, but your voice isn't giving you away right now. Is that a 'good' busy?"

"It's more of an 'I'm not sure what I'm doing' busy, Mom. I've been spending a lot of time with Nathan."

"Oh, really?" Tracy knew her mom and knew she was trying to sound nonchalant. Laura didn't fool her for a minute.

"Yes, really. But don't get too excited. He lives in Wentworth Cove and I live in Boston. Remember?"

"I'm not excited. Do I sound excited? Just a detached curiosity. That's all. So satisfy my mild curiosity and tell me all about it."

"Well, we spent the morning sailing, and Wednesday I drove up to Camden with him. He writes copy for a clothing company and had to pick up some clothes at the headquarters."

"Sounds interesting. Keep me posted. Have you met anyone else?"

"Not really." This was not the time, Tracy felt, to bring up having lunch with John. "How's Molly, and how's everything in Boston?"

"It's been warm here, but Molly's fine, of course. She was asking about you a day or two ago, in fact. What do you do all day, Trace? Has it been difficult to wind down?"

"Not as bad as I thought it would be. I've read a little, cooked a little, explored a little. Kate had me over for dinner one night with her family."

"Isn't that Nathan's mother? Is she trying to play matchmaker?"

"No, I don't think so. She's just really friendly."

"That's nice. I'd like to meet these new friends of yours sometime."

"I don't know, Mom. I'll probably never see them again after I leave in a couple of weeks."

"I trust you to make the right decisions, but remember that sometimes people cross our paths for a reason, and it would be a shame to walk away from something or someone that could have brought happiness to your life. All I'm saying is don't burn any bridges when you leave Wentworth Cove. You might be sorry afterward."

Those words stung Tracy, and she couldn't respond for a moment. When she regained her composure, she said, "No, I won't. Well, I guess I'd better go now. Hug Molly for me. I'll talk to you again in a few days."

"Okay. I'm glad you called. Have fun."

Tracy turned her phone off, put it on the charger, and walked outside. Sinking down into one of the two Adirondack chairs in the backyard, she pulled her knees up to her chest and hot tears began to stream down her cheeks. *It's even more obvious now than before, but I just can't bring myself to talk to her about it.*

Tracy didn't know how to cope with the realization that her mother had been unfaithful to her dad, that he probably had known, and that John Strong, not Kenneth Ratcliffe, was her biological father. She considered going to Nathan's, but she wasn't ready to pull him into this. For some reason, she thought it would complicate their relationship. No, she needed to keep John and Nathan separate issues in her life. For the time being, at least.

Chapter Fourteen

Sunday morning broke with magnificent beams of sunshine pouring through the bedroom window. Although it had been years since Tracy had been to church, she had promised Nathan she would go with him this morning.

There was a time when spiritual matters and going to church had played a major role in her life. But those days were over. She had drifted away several years ago and hadn't seen much of a reason to go back, relegating the faith of her earlier years to the past.

She figured it wouldn't hurt, though—just this once—to go with Nathan and his family to Wentworth Cove Community Church. She'd noticed it on her drive into town for food and every time she went to Kennebunk.

It was a charming stone structure that seemed to belong more in a Thomas Kinkade painting than along the side of a highway. Set back in a grove of sea pines, the church did have an inviting look to it, though, and Tracy had wondered what kind of people would abandon a comfortable cottage on a Sunday morning to go there.

As they walked in, she immediately spotted Jessica motioning them over. Seated on the third pew from the front were the rest of the Norsworthy family. Did they really have to sit that close to the front? Even when she *did* attend church services, she sat as close to the back as possible so she could slip out without having to speak to anyone. She slid in beside Elizabeth, and even though they had met only once, Elizabeth squeezed her hand gently and whispered, "I'm glad you came today. I know it means a lot to Nathan."

The organ prelude began, and the chords of "Holy, Holy, Holy" caused the sanctuary to take on an air of reverence. After everyone sang a few hymns, the minister began to speak. His voice was deep and resonant, easy to listen to, and before Tracy knew it, an hour had passed and they were standing to leave.

"Hi, Tracy." It was Maggie, and Annie was standing behind her. "Annie told me she saw you the other day. How've you been?"

"Fine. You? How're things at the bookstore?"

"Everything's good. Bernard's been away quite a bit, though, and I've had to hold down the fort by myself. His mother isn't doing well, and he's been spending most of his time with her. He's hired a nurse, but he wants to spend as much time as possible with her, too."

Of course, Maggie didn't know that Tracy had met Nora Solomon, and she had no intention of telling her. "She's the one who works crossword puzzles in ink, isn't she? I'm sorry to hear she's ill."

Annie had engaged Nathan in a conversation, but as soon as he could, he made an excuse to go, and they went to eat with Kate, David, Elizabeth and Jessica at Seascapes, the only restaurant in Wentworth Cove Tracy hadn't tried.

After she got back to the cottage, she spent the rest of the afternoon curled up in the rose covered chair reading and thinking about Nathan.

Chapter Fifteen

Monday morning Tracy slept late and decided to go for a walk along the shore. But when she opened the front door, her eyes spotted a white envelope pushed halfway under the doormat. Her name was on the envelope, but she didn't recognize the handwriting. Who would have left her a letter rather than knocking on the door? John was the only person she could think of, and immediately that same sick feeling she had experienced so many times when she thought of him visited her again in the pit of her stomach. Did she want to know what the letter said? Was she ready? But if she chose not to open it, could she live with not knowing?

Her fingers trembled as they slowly and carefully ripped open the envelope and pulled out the letter.

Dear Tracy,

I'm very sorry to have to be the one to tell you this, but I think you deserve to know, and there is no one else who knows and can tell you. I'm writing this in a letter because I wanted to give you time to process the information by yourself without anyone else around.

I don't know how serious you feel that your relationship with Nathan is at this point, but since you are leaving Wentworth Cove in a week or two and could be making some serious decisions soon, I think you deserve to know the truth. I liked you the first day we met and don't want you to be deceived.

As you probably remember, I have known Nathan for many years, and in those years we've developed a very close friendship. He has confided in me several times about things that are important to him, but this is something I wish he hadn't told me. Since he did, however, I think you should know, too.

I'm sure you know he's almost finished with a novel that he's been working on for a couple of years. This afternoon he told me that he hopes to be able to get his foot in the door of a publishing company through you. I was surprised and asked him if he would really use you like that, but he said he didn't see it that way. He said you'd be leaving in a couple of weeks anyway, and you weren't expecting anything from him.

Anyway, I'm sorry, Tracy, if you had strong feelings for him, but I thought it was better that you find out now before things went any further.

Maggie

P.S. Please don't let him know I told you. Remember, I have to live here after you leave.

All of a sudden that walk didn't seem so appealing. Tracy tried to dismiss what Maggie's letter said, but it wasn't that easy. Maggie had never given Tracy any reason to think she was out to get Nathan for herself. But on the other hand, she hadn't known Maggie long. As a matter of fact, she hadn't known Nathan long either, and the more she pondered those two unsettling thoughts, the more upset she became.

Although she didn't know where she was going, Tracy felt an urgent need to get away from Wentworth Cove. She threw some things in an overnight bag, locked up the cottage, jumped in her car and started driving. Not away from the ocean—she wasn't ready to leave it yet. Not back toward Boston—she didn't want to go home and face her mother with so many questions about John still unanswered. So she drove north, up the coast on Highway 1, the same route she'd taken with Nathan less than a week, and what seemed like a lifetime, ago. Biddeford, Portland, Brunswick. She kept driving. Newcastle, Rockland.

Looking out the windshield at a tear-blurred landscape, she felt as alone as she had ever felt in her life. This vacation that was to have been a time for her to relax had turned into a nightmare.

Gina. She had to talk to Gina. By the time she reached Camden, she'd vowed she would not return to Wentworth Cove, for any reason. Someone else would have to pack the rest of her clothes and turn in the key to the Graysons. Gina would do that for her. If not, she would just mail it in and leave her clothes. Nothing would get her back to that cottage. Back to that village.

Tracy pulled up in front of the first bed and breakfast she saw after following the road into downtown Camden. A tall, thin man with a rough, weatherworn face and a large, hooked nose met her at the door. He looked as much like Ichabod Crane as anyone she'd ever seen.

"I was wondering if I could get a room for a couple of nights—maybe longer." How long would she stay in Camden? She really had no idea. At this point, the future was a complete unknown.

"Nope. Full up here. It's tourist season, in case you hadn't noticed. Don't expect you'll be finding anything in

Camden. Maybe on up the road a bit. Maybe not."

"Thank you," Tracy said, more out of habit than sincerity and walked back to her car not knowing what she was going to do.

Gina would have to do her thinking for her. She dialed Gina's number. *Please answer your phone.*

"Hello."

"Gina. Thank goodness. I'm glad you're home."

"Tracy, what's wrong? You don't sound like yourself."

"My world just fell apart, but other than that, I'm quite all right," Tracy managed to get out, choking back tears.

"You might as well go ahead and tell me what happened. You know I'll get it out of you sooner or later anyway. I have all the time in the world. Todd's at work, and Hunter's occupied with *Sesame Street.*"

"You know I wouldn't ask you this if I weren't desperate, but could you possibly get away and come up here? I'm in Camden."

"Camden? You left Wentworth Cove? What are you doing in Camden?"

"Not much, really. I haven't eaten anything all day, and I can't find a place to stay. This town is packed with tourists, and I don't know where else to go. I guess I'll just get back on Highway 1 and head north again until I find a place to stay. If you can't come, I'll totally understand. I know you have Todd and Hunter to think about first."

"Hold on. Don't start making my plans for me. I'm quite capable of doing that myself. Todd will be fine for a couple of days, and Marian has been asking me when I'm going to bring her grandson to Portsmouth for a few days. Let me make a couple of phone calls, and I'll call you back."

"Gina, I don't even know where I'm going to stay tonight. There's apparently nothing here in Camden."

"Stay put for a while and leave everything to me, Trace. Todd has a cousin in Camden. I'll see what I can do. Keep your phone turned on. And meanwhile, go get something to eat. Do they have pizza there? If I recall correctly, you could always eat pizza, no matter what was going on in your life. How about it?"

"I'll try."

Not even pizza sounded appealing. Rather than driving back downtown and trying to find a place to park, she decided to walk—past the library, past the harbor, past a corner market.

Comfort food. She needed it again. Clam chowder. Where could she get a bowl of clam chowder? Then she spotted it. Dockside Café. Perfect. She was halfway through the bowl of chowder when her phone rang.

"Hey, where are you right now?" Gina asked.

"I'm eating like you told me to."

"Good. But I mean where? Are you still in Camden?"

"Yes, I'm at Dockside Café on High Street. Why?"

"I just talked to Todd's cousin Lucas, and he says we can stay with him as long as we need to. He has a spare bedroom because his son's in Bangor for the month with his mom."

"I don't know, Gina…"

"Tracy, as I see it, you don't have much of a choice, do you? You don't want to go back to Wentworth Cove. You don't want to go back to Boston. You don't have a place to stay in Camden. Now *you* tell *me* what you plan to do."

"Of course. You're right. I just don't want to be around people right now, and I don't even know Lucas. Did I meet him at the wedding?"

"Probably, but I don't know for sure. He was married then, but his wife left him a couple of years ago. He has custody of his son, but as I said, Jake's with his mom in Bangor for the month of July, so his room is empty. I've never been to his house, but it'll be a bed and a roof over your head anyway. Our heads, that is. I'm packing a bag for Hunter and one for me, and I've already called Todd and Marian. Todd sends his love. What do you say?"

"I guess I say okay. As you said, I don't have much of a choice, do I?"

"No, you don't. So here's what you do. It'll take me about five hours to get there. Do you know where the library is? Lucas said it's on Main Street."

"Yeah. I passed it on my way into town."

"Try to be there by four-thirty or five. I'll meet you and Lucas there. He'll probably get to the library before I do. He said he'll try to leave work around four."

"Thanks, Gina. Don't get a speeding ticket, but please hurry. I don't feel like baring my soul to a perfect stranger, even if he is Todd's cousin."

"Hang in there. I'm on my way."

"Gina, wait a minute. How will I recognize Lucas?"

"Oh, don't worry about that. He said he remembers you from our wedding. Apparently he was pretty impressed by my 'beautiful, blonde maid of honor.'"

Chapter Sixteen

Tracy wound her way through the streets of Camden, passing candle stores, antique stores, coffee shops and eateries, in what proved to be a futile attempt to purge Wentworth Cove and all that happened there from her mind. Unable to run from the memories and getting no satisfaction from browsing the quaint little shops, she resigned herself to going to the library a full two hours before she was supposed to meet Lucas and Gina.

After all, she mused, her life was measured in libraries, wasn't it? The library of her childhood, the one her mother now presided over. She had grown up there, reading everything from Beatrix Potter and Lewis Carroll to William Faulkner and James Joyce. The high school library where she had effectively hidden from normal teenage life for four years. The library at Boston College, her safe haven away from the chaotic madness of dorm life. John's library in Kennebunk, representing the chapter in her life that she was so desperately attempting to get away from.

And now the library in Camden—representing what? The unknown? Where was she going from here? How had she gotten into this mess? Just a few weeks ago she was a relatively satisfied literary agent at a prestigious agency in Boston, hoping to spend a few weeks away from the city, then go home refreshed, eyes rested, brain rested, ready to work again.

Now she was standing on a street in a town where she knew no one, watching tourists file off a bus in front of her, wondering where they came from, where they were going, and if any of them had ever felt as alone as she did right now. She shuffled along behind them for a couple of blocks, and when they turned to walk down to the harbor, she headed for the library.

Tracy picked up an Agatha Christie, asked the librarian if there was a quiet reading room, and vowed to spend a couple of hours helping Miss Marple solve one of her myriad mysteries.

But the more she tried to keep her mind on the book, the more she realized her inability to run from the memories of Wentworth Cove. She had always been known at work as the queen of pragmatism, but now her mind was nothing but mush. Her feelings for Nathan were ambivalent, ranging from an intense desire to run back to him and throw her arms around his tall, lanky body to a burning need to confront him with her newfound knowledge of his intent, his duplicity.

She managed to read a while longer before glancing at her watch. Four o'clock. Mercifully, over an hour had passed in spite of her intermittent reading and tormented musings.

Just then she looked up and saw a man ambling toward her. He was wearing khaki slacks, a light blue oxford shirt and a navy blazer, as tall as Nathan but broader in the shoulders, his close cropped hair a light, sandy brown, his blue eyes fixed on Tracy. A sideways grin lit up his face as he approached her and stuck out his hand.

"Hi, Tracy. You probably don't remember me from Todd and Gina's wedding, but I'm Lucas, Todd's cousin. Welcome to Camden."

"I'm sorry, but there were so many people at the wedding, and I was so—"

"Don't apologize. I understand totally. You were quite busy with your maid-of-honor duties, and I was married at the time, or I'm sure I would have made my presence known to you." There was that sideways grin again. Charming.

Tracy actually did remember him—remembered seeing him anyway. He was the kind of person who would not be easy to miss, about six feet tall with muscles that seemed to ripple even under a sport coat. Tracy and Gina had always rated men on a one to ten scale with ten being drop-dead gorgeous. Tracy figured he was about a nine point eight. *I can't believe Gina didn't mention how good-looking he is.*

"Thank you for letting us stay with you. I don't know what I was thinking, driving up here without reservations during the height of tourist season. Actually, I wasn't thinking at all the time. That was the problem."

"Your loss of rationality is my gain. I'll enjoy the company. My son is with his mother for the month, and it gets rather lonesome sometimes when he's not around."

"How old is he?" Tracy asked.

"Jake's seven. Karen was pregnant with him at Todd and Gina's wedding. After he was born, things went downhill for us. We divorced when he was two."

"And you have full custody?" Tracy hoped she wasn't being too nosy, but he didn't seem to mind talking about it.

"Yeah, Karen's the one who asked for the divorce. Said she didn't want to be married anymore. Of course, you can't really divorce a kid, but she would have if I had let

118

her. I made her a deal that if she would agree to stay in his life and see him once a month and a full month each summer, I wouldn't ask for any child support. It was just as well. She can barely support herself. All beauty and no brains. I should have thought of that before we got married, but I wasn't thinking with my head back in those days."

"I appreciate your getting off early to rescue me. Where do you work?"

"I'm an attorney with a small firm here in Camden—Seymour, Lane & Koch. How about you?"

"I'm an agent with Smithson Literary Agency in Boston." Tracy breathed a silent prayer that he wasn't trying to be the next John Grisham, in the process of writing a book and needing a literary agent. She'd had all of that she could take on this vacation.

"Could I interest you in a cup of coffee or tea? There's a coffee shop just around the corner. I'll tell the librarian to be on the lookout for Gina and send her over."

"That sounds wonderful."

Mingled scents of coffee, chocolate, and biscotti greeted them as Lucas held the door for her. Although the room was crowded, Tracy managed to find a table while he stood in line.

It was the first really torpid day of summer, but the steaming cup of cappuccino Lucas set in front of her a few minutes later looked and smelled delicious. Just the thing to calm her nerves.

"I'm really sorry I haven't kept up with Todd and Gina since the wedding," Lucas was saying as he pulled out his chair and sat down. "The distance, I guess, coupled with the divorce. I get down to Boston on business sometimes but never to Vermont."

"To Boston? What kind of business do you usually have there?"

"I was there about six months ago, February, I think it was. One of my clients has a business in Boston. Next time I'm down, I'll have to look you up. That is, if it's okay with you."

"Sure. That would be nice. Maybe Todd and Gina could drive down and join us."

When Lucas's face dropped at her suggestion, Tracy realized a family reunion wasn't what he had in mind at all.

Chapter Seventeen

Finally, Gina burst through the door, breathless as usual. "I'm sorry it took me so long to get here. I thought I'd never get away from Marian. Hi, Lucas. It's good to see you. Todd sends his regards. Tracy, honey. How are you?" Gina asked, hugging her friend.

"Better than I was when I talked to you last. Thank you so much for coming."

"I'm starving," Gina said. Gina was always starving. "How about you two?"

"I already had plans for this evening before you called, and I know you two have a lot to talk about anyway, so I'm going to give you directions to my house, tell you where the spare key is hidden, and meet you there later. Gina, there are lots of good restaurants in this general area. Do you need any suggestions?"

"Tracy," Gina asked, "are you hungry for anything special?

"No, I'm fine with anything."

"Thanks, Lucas. We'll just wander around until we find something that looks good. We'll see you at your house sometime tonight then."

Lucas handed them a map he had hastily drawn on a napkin, told them his key was under a flowerpot by the back door, and left.

"Tracy," Gina began as soon as he was out the door, "what on earth is going on? Did you find out something else about the man who knew your mother years ago?"

"No, it's not that. Well… it is that, but not only that. Remember when you told me not to mess things up with Nathan?"

"I didn't remember his name, but I do remember telling you that. Why?"

"Well, I took your advice. I didn't mess things up, but…" Tracy paused, unable to put her feelings into words, even to Gina.

"But what? Trace, don't leave me hanging like this. What happened?"

"I fell in love with him." She hadn't expressed it, hadn't realized it, until that moment.

"Yeah? Yeah? That's good news. So what's the problem?" Gina thought love conquered all, so how could there possibly be a problem?

"This morning I found a letter tucked under my doormat from a friend of his advising me that he was using me to get to a publisher. He's working on a manuscript."

"Male or female friend?"

"Female."

"Aha."

"Aha, what?"

"How well do you know this so-called friend, and why would you believe her? I can think of all sorts of reasons someone would tell you that. He's a ten, right?"

"Twelve. Why?"

"Have you talked to Nathan about the letter?"

"Of course not. I couldn't. I just left."

"Tracy, honestly. Sometimes you exasperate me. Do you know that? You really do. First, you think your mother had an affair and your dad isn't your real dad, but you won't talk to her about it. Then you fall in love with this guy—something I had almost given up hope on, by the way—and this happens, and you tell me you haven't talked to him either. How do you ever know who to believe if you never give anyone a chance to explain anything to you?"

"Gina, really. I called you because I needed someone to talk to, not someone to scold me. There are plenty of people I could have called for that."

"I'm sorry. I guess it's just that you don't handle things the way I do. I've always been more direct than you. I'm here because you're my dearest friend in the world, and I care what happens to you. I hope you know that. But honestly, why don't you just confront him with the accusation? Tell him you know."

"Because Maggie asked me not to. They've been friends for a long time, and she has to live in the same town with him when I leave."

"Honestly. You are *so* naïve."

"No, Gina," Tracy protested. "You don't know the whole situation. Maggie's not like that. She befriended me when I first arrived in Wentworth Cove—asked me to the Fourth of July parade and fireworks display when she knew he'd be there. If she wanted him for herself, why would she take a chance like that?"

"I don't know the answer to that one, but I do know that you've been running from emotional involvement all your life. Don't you think it's time to stop and face some situations, and some people?"

"Let's go eat, and I'll promise to think about it. Come on. My treat. It's the least I can do after you drove all the way up here to chide me," Tracy teased as she hugged her friend.

After they'd enjoyed shrimp scampi at the Waterview Restaurant, Gina drove Tracy to her car, which was still parked in front of the bed and breakfast. Tracy took the map on a napkin and led the way to Lucas's house. Gina had always been directionally challenged.

The house was an eclectic blend of shabby chic and early marriage retro, and it was evident Lucas was not expecting company anytime soon. Gina and Tracy talked for a couple of hours and, deciding Lucas was planning to make it a late night, found what was obviously his son's bedroom—replete with twin beds, plaid wallpaper and baseball posters—and went to bed.

Tracy slept fitfully, tossing and turning, waking up, it seemed, every few minutes. Finally, at five-thirty, when she couldn't stay in bed any longer, she quietly put on her robe and slipped into the kitchen, hoping to find some coffee and a coffee maker.

"Well, hello. What got you up so early? This is the middle of the night for most people." Lucas had already made a pot of coffee and was sitting at the table reading *The Wall Street Journal.*

"I guess it's because Gina and I went to bed so early last night. I'm usually okay on six or seven hours."

"How about a cup of java?" Lucas asked, getting up and pulling out a chair. He poured Tracy a cup and set it in front of her.

"Looks good. Smells good, too. Just what I need this morning. Thanks for letting us stay here on such short notice. You're a lifesaver. I don't know what I would have done if Gina hadn't thought of this."

"Tracy, I don't want to pry, but when Gina called, she said something about a problem you had down in Wentworth Cove. Is it something I could help with? If it's a legal problem, I'm at your service. Corporate law is my specialty, but I've been known to bail some of my friends out of some pretty sticky situations. If it's something else, I don't know if I can do anything to help, but I am a good listener, believe it or not."

He sounded so sincere that Tracy felt comfortable telling him a little bit about Nathan. She tried to laugh it off and make light of the situation, but she was sure he saw through her effort.

Laying his hand on hers, he spoke. "I can understand, to a degree, what you must be feeling. Karen left me, and I didn't know which end was up for several months. She really pulled the rug out from under me when she announced she wanted a divorce. It came totally out of the blue."

"I'm sorry," was all Tracy could think of to say.

"Don't be. I realize now that it was for the best. Although I'd rather raise Jake in a two-parent family, we get along quite well. And I haven't let myself get lonesome, if you know what I mean."

Before she realized what was happening, Lucas had moved his chair closer to Tracy's and was rubbing her arm.

"You shouldn't let yourself be lonely either—someone as beautiful as you," he said, putting his arm around her shoulder.

"Lucas, no, I'm not ready…" she protested.

"You should be. I can help you forget about what happened to you in Wentworth Cove. Let me at least try. You won't regret it."

"No, I don't…" Tracy began as his grip tightened around her.

Instead of feeling comforted by him, she felt repulsed. Her disgust was intensifying with each second as she struggled to pull away, but rather than release her, he grabbed her and pulled her closer, his warm breath now on her face, nauseating her with its closeness. With every bit of strength she could muster, she jerked herself away from him and out of his grip.

"Lucas, if you feel I owe you something for your hospitality, I'll be glad to pay, but I won't pay that way."

"You misunderstood me totally. I'm not looking for any kind of payment. I just wanted to help you forget those problems you were running from, that guy in Wentworth Cove who hurt you. I would never hurt you like that."

"Well, if you really want to help, you'll let me get over this in my own way. It'll take some time."

"Okay. I'll tell you what. I have to go into the office early today. I'll meet you back here around five o'clock. Then we can talk some more. How about it?"

"We'll see," she mumbled as she watched him swagger out the door, knowing she would never let herself be alone in the same room with him again. The conversation he was planning for tonight would never take place. Lucas was a time bomb, and she didn't intend to be the one to detonate him.

Tracy slipped into the shower, careful not to wake Gina, but feeling the need to wash away the hopelessness she felt. She stood there for what seemed like hours luxuriating in the feeling of the hot water removing the grime of what had happened in the kitchen. Even if he was Todd's cousin, she certainly had no intention of allowing him to use her to satisfy his ego. She wasn't that vulnerable. In fact, the more she thought about it, the less vulnerable she felt.

Maybe Gina was right. Maybe she should stop running from life. That was, after all, what she had been doing for as long as she could remember.

When Tracy tiptoed back into the bedroom, Gina was just beginning to stir. "Tracy, what are you doing up so early? You've already showered? You haven't broken that bad habit of getting up at the crack of dawn, yet?"

"I didn't sleep very well," Tracy answered.

"Well, I sure did. Slept like a baby. What do you want to do today? Look around Camden some more? Go up to Bar Harbor?"

"No, I think I'm ready to go back to Wentworth Cove."

"You're what?" Gina asked in exasperation. "I thought I heard you say you're ready to go back to Wentworth Cove."

Tracy told her about what had happened in the kitchen with Lucas, that she didn't want to be there when he got home at five, and that she was ready to go back and try to get some situations cleared up.

This revelation apparently pleased Gina immensely because she jumped out of bed and into the shower, shouting behind her, "It's a good thing I have a child. I've learned how to be ready in thirty minutes. Get your stuff packed up. Breakfast is on me!"

Chapter Eighteen

The drive back to Wentworth Cove was fraught with emotions. Though still upset by Maggie's revelation about Nathan, Tracy was determined to get to the heart of the matter about John and her mother. *What happened that summer while my dad was at Oxford? What could possibly have caused my mother to betray a man who was so perfect? What kind of a man was John? Why had he pursued a married woman?*

Gina followed close behind in her red Saab, and when they stopped for lunch, they talked about possibilities. Gina was as much of a doer as Tracy was a thinker. "Get out of your head, Tracy," she often said, "and just do something." Easy for her to say.

"When we get back," she advised, "I want you to go to see Nathan and get that all cleared up. Confront him and see what he has to say for himself."

"And what do I do if he completely denies saying anything like that to Maggie?"

"Then you have to weigh the evidence. How much do you trust Maggie? How much do you trust Nathan? Which one do you feel like you know better?"

"I *thought* I knew Nathan," Tracy answered. *But then I thought I knew my mother, too, didn't I?*

"Didn't you tell me that Maggie had a thing for him at one time? Maybe it's not over for her. No matter how much she protests. Maybe she's just trying to save face." Gina. Ever the optimist. To her, life would always be a fairy tale.

"Gina, you're a Pollyanna, but I love you for that, among other things. But what works for you doesn't work for me. I think I'll try to talk to Maggie first. Will you come with me?"

"Of course, I will. What do you think I'm here for? And since I'm much better at reading people than you are, I'll let you know whether she's lying or not." Gina absentmindedly and repeatedly tucked her hair behind her left ear, a gesture that Tracy knew meant she was as deep in thought as Gina ever got. "But what about your mother? Do you have a grand plan for tackling that situation?"

"Not really. But one crisis at a time, if you don't mind. That's all I can take right now."

They made plans to see Maggie at work the next morning, got back in their cars and continued driving until they reached Wentworth Cove and Grayson Cottage. Not wanting Nathan to know she was back, Tracy led Gina two blocks down and around the corner to park their cars. Then they walked to the cottage. The sun, now well advanced, shone on the flowers in the window boxes and along the walkway to the door.

"What a cute little house!" Most houses were little to Gina, now that she and Todd, planning to expand their family soon, had moved into a five-bedroom, two-story Colonial. Tracy thought about Gina and Todd and Hunter.

She'd never before wanted what Gina had. Satisfied with her career, she hadn't been tempted to let her thoughts stray to marriage and a family. So why was she thinking about those things now? What had changed? If she wanted to be honest, she'd have to admit it had something to do with meeting Nathan. In fact, it had everything to do with meeting Nathan.

Well, then why does it hurt so badly? People don't die of a broken heart. Get a grip, Tracy. You've always been able to do that. And if you ever needed to take control of your emotions, this is the time.

After another night of tossing and turning, morning broke with sunlight streaming in through lace curtains that billowed in the breeze. The aroma of coffee filled Tracy's nostrils as she realized that Gina had actually beaten her to the kitchen.

"Good morning. Thought you might need a jumpstart with a little java. I slept like a baby with the window open. Must have been the sea breeze. I haven't smelled air like that in a long time. I think when I get back home I'll try to talk Todd into taking a vacation. Doubt I'll have much luck, though. He seems to actually like working. Go figure. How'd you sleep?"

"You're unusually wide awake this morning. What woke you? And to answer your question, I didn't sleep very well again. Kept waking up and having trouble going back to sleep. Couldn't get my thoughts off what I have to do today."

Gina poured Tracy a cup of coffee, and they sat down at the table to plan their strategy.

"You know," Gina started, "I'm more insightful than you give me credit for. I've been thinking about this, and I've come to the conclusion that you need to call your mom soon. I think I know her pretty well, and I know you can talk to her about anything. Just ask her if she knows John. What's his last name?"

Tracy drew a slow, deep, calming breath. "Strong. But Gina—"

"No. Hear me out. Wouldn't you feel more like sorting out this thing with Nathan if you knew the truth about John?"

Tracy gazed into Gina's kind blue eyes. Gina had always been there for her, had always wanted the best for her, and Tracy treasured her friendship, but didn't she realize that Tracy's life was unraveling right here, right now? How could she possibly understand the immensity of the conflicted feelings Tracy had for her mother?

It was ironic, wasn't it? After a few years of just tolerating each other—at least that's the way Tracy saw it—they had finally developed that closeness that many of her friends had with their mothers. And now? Tracy wondered what would be left of their relationship after they talked about John. If it wasn't true, Tracy would have accused her of being unfaithful to her husband. If it was… well…

"I appreciate you for leaving Todd and Hunter and coming all this way to rescue me. I really do… but I have to do this my way." Tracy swallowed hard to rid her throat of the ten-pound lump that had invaded it. "And I'm going to see Maggie today. She'll be at work, but she won't mind. That's where I first met her."

"Okay. You obviously have your mind made up, and I know when I'm beaten. Let's get ready and get it over with. What time does she get to work?"

"I think Bernie's shop opens at nine."

"Well," Gina conceded, glancing at her watch, "we have an hour to get ready. Let's go."

131

Chapter Nineteen

Bernard's Books and Collectibles was teeming with customers when they walked in at ten minutes after nine—a scenario Tracy hadn't anticipated. Maggie was tall, and Tracy quickly spotted her behind the counter and waved.

"Hi, Tracy. I'll be with you in a minute." She couldn't read anything, one way or the other, in Maggie's greeting.

"That's okay. I just want you to meet my friend Gina, and I'd like to talk to you when you have time."

"Great. But it won't be until we close at six. Bernie's mother is sick, and he'll be with her today. I brought my lunch so I can watch the store all day. It seems tourist season has hit as you can see. Excuse me a minute."

She continued checking out customers, and Gina and Tracy walked away to talk about Plan B.

"We could either wait around for all the people to leave and try to talk to her then," Gina proposed, "but someone else might walk in. Or we could see if we can take her to dinner when she gets off at six. Can you wait that long to find out?"

"I guess I'll have to, won't I? It seems I don't have much control over my life anymore."

Although they had driven to the bookstore in Gina's car, Tracy wanted to leave as quickly as possible since the art gallery was just down the street, and she wasn't ready to see Nathan, yet. They made arrangements to pick Maggie up at six and drove back to the cottage.

"Well, what would you like to do today?" Tracy inquired. "You might as well make this a mini-vacation since you're stuck here for at least another day."

Since they couldn't go to the beach, which Tracy had come to realize was one of Nathan's favorite haunts, Gina opted to go shopping in Kennebunkport. Now she just hoped they wouldn't run into John. For someone who had been in Maine only two and a half weeks, she already knew two too many people.

The day was interminably long, but six o'clock finally came, and they headed for the bookstore in Gina's car again. Maggie was just locking up as they pulled up to the front of the store.

"Hi, I'm Gina, Tracy's friend for—well, let's just say lots and lots of years."

Did Tracy detect a hint of possessiveness in her tone? Was she trying to make a point here? Don't you dare hurt my friend… or something like that?

"I'm Maggie and I'm glad to meet you. I didn't know Tracy had a friend coming to see her while she's here."

"Well, it wasn't exactly planned, but she was having so much fun that I just decided to join her."

Fortunately, Gina was carrying the conversation, and Tracy wouldn't have to say much until they got to the restaurant. Tracy was once again thankful for having her best friend there with her.

"Maggie," Tracy started finally when their drinks had arrived, "I need to ask you something, and I'm hoping you'll be completely honest with me. I don't have any reason to think you won't. It's just that this is something that's been bothering me for a couple of days." Tracy twisted restlessly in her chair. "Do you have any idea what it could be?"

Maggie looked from Tracy to Gina and back to Tracy again. "Of course I don't, Tracy, but ask away. I don't have any reason *not* to be honest with you. Is this about Nathan?"

"So it's true, then."

"What's true?"

"The letter."

"Now I'm afraid I don't know what you're talking about. What letter?"

Tracy slowly pulled the letter from her purse and handed it to Maggie. As she read it, Tracy tried to read her expression, but outwardly Maggie kept her composure. "I'll kill her. I swear I'll kill her the next time I see her." And all of a sudden it all made sense. Not Maggie, but Annie. Annie had written the letter and signed Maggie's name. She was the one who was so jealous of Nathan, and it wasn't true. Nothing in the letter was true.

"I'm sorry, Maggie, but I had to find out."

"You have nothing to apologize for. I'm the one who's sorry Annie put you through this. She's done it before, you know. I don't mean she's signed my name. That's a first. But when Jessica, Nathan's niece, started dating Tim Grayson, she wrote Tim an anonymous letter saying all sorts of untrue things about Jessica. And a sweeter girl than Jess you'd never want to meet. Well, it was typed, and she never admitted it, but she had liked Tim for a long time, so I think everyone knew she did it. Fortunately, they got it all straightened out before it caused any lasting damage to that relationship."

Tracy's mind flashed back to a scene at the beach on the Fourth when they all three ran into each other. She thought the air was a little chilly for a summer night, and now this revelation brought that incident into focus for her.

Finally, their dinner came and Tracy's appetite was fully restored. They ate their grilled chicken Caesars amid small talk, mostly between Gina and Maggie. Tracy's thoughts were on Nathan. Had he tried to see her while she'd been gone? What would she tell him about her impromptu little jaunt up the coast? No need to mention the letter—or Annie—Tracy decided. Maggie was already infuriated, not to mention embarrassed, by her conniving sister.

"Do you realize how exciting this is?" Gina asked as soon as they dropped Maggie at her car. "When do I get to meet Mr. Wonderful?"

"Whoa, kiddo. I think I need to see him first and try to explain where I've been in case he's tried to see me in the last couple of days."

"Fine. You know where he lives, right? Then let's go."

"I mean alone."

"Oh. Of course. Do you want me to take you to your car and wait at the cottage?"

"Sure. But Gina?"

"What?"

"I'm a little nervous."

"Great. That's a good sign. Calm, cool, collected Tracy Ratcliffe, nervous about a guy. You don't know how happy that makes me."

"Well, since you're in such a joyous mood, why don't you try to think of something I can tell Nathan to explain where I've been for two and a half days."

"I think the truth usually works best in cases like this."

Tracy knew Gina was right about this one. A relationship that wasn't based on truth wasn't much of a relationship at all.

This time they pulled both cars directly in front of the cottage, announcing to all that she was back. If Nathan happened to drive by, he'd know.

As long as she could remember, dusk had been her favorite time of day. The busyness of the day was giving way to the gloaming. This summer evening was no different. Much had happened, much had been resolved, but there was still something she had to do.

"Tracy... Tracy. Did you hear anything I just said? Where's your key? Are you coming in or not?"

"Yeah. For a minute. I think I'll change clothes."

"Tracy Ratcliffe changes clothes for a man. What *is* this world coming to? I'll know you're really serious when you start cooking for him."

What Gina didn't know wouldn't hurt her.

Tracy walked in, flipped on the light, and stopped, astonished. She couldn't believe what she saw. On the coffee table sat a crystal vase full of pink roses. A folded piece of paper lay beside them. Her heart beat a little faster as she wondered how someone could have gained entrance to the cottage. Ever so slowly she opened and read the note.

I've missed you. Nathan.

"Tracy, that's so romantic," Gina exclaimed. "I can't wait to meet this guy."

"Make yourself at home," Tracy called, looking back, as she grabbed her keys and ran out the front door.

Since she'd never been to Nathan's apartment, and the art gallery was closed for the evening, Tracy walked around to the back door. Nathan flung it open before she had a chance to knock. Oh, but he looked good, dressed in jeans and a white T-shirt. His hair was a bit messed up, as if he had just taken a nap and hadn't looked in the mirror since waking.

"I thought that was your car I saw out the window. I hoped that was your car I saw out the window. You don't owe me any explanations, but I just want you to know I missed you terribly. I didn't know I could miss anyone so much, and I was afraid something happened and you had gone back to Boston."

"Something did happen, and I'll tell you all about it soon, but I'm back now. And thanks for the roses. They're beautiful. By the way, how'd you get in? Did I leave the door unlocked?"

"Did you forget? I have connections. Jess? Tim?"

"I see—a conspiracy. I guess I'll forgive them, but only because I love roses. Pink roses, specifically," Tracy said, smiling.

As if on cue, Nathan enveloped her in his arms and held her close for a long time. He seemed to think she might leave again and he had to do something physical to prevent it. But she had no desire to leave—until she had to—and she didn't want to think about that day right now.

"Are you busy?" she asked him. "There's someone I want you to meet."

"Who is it? There's someone here you know and I don't?"

"There is now. Come on. She's dying to meet you. I'll bring you back."

"Did your mother come up?"

"No."

"Who then?"

"You'll see. I think I'll keep you in suspense until we get there. This is fun."

The tires screeched and flung gravel as Tracy pulled up in front of the cottage a little too hastily. Nathan looked at her quizzically as they followed the curved path up to the front door. When Gina opened the door, Tracy could tell by the look on her face that she approved.

"Nathan, this is Gina, my college roommate and my dearest friend."

"Well, this is a surprise and a pleasure. Tracy didn't tell me you were coming."

"She didn't exactly know. It was kind of a surprise to her, too." Gina eyed her quizzically, not knowing how much she had told him.

"I haven't told him the whole story yet. I will later," Tracy assured her.

They talked until midnight. What was it about Gina that put everyone at ease? There was none of the shyness she'd seen in Nathan when she first met him. Was it Gina's easygoing personality, or was it that he felt so comfortable with Tracy now, and that carried over to her friend. Whatever it was, she liked it. Liked the feel of having someone. Someone Gina so obviously approved of. Before she drove him back to the gallery, they had made arrangements for Gina to meet the whole Norsworthy family the next day.

The next day. Tracy knew what she had to do the next day. She had to call her mother, and to say she wasn't looking forward to it was the understatement of the century.

Chapter Twenty

Tracy rose before Gina, dressed quickly and quietly, grabbed her phone, and walked out into the backyard, determined to get it over with. Tackling the situation head on was the way to go, she decided. At least the problem with the letter had worked out well. Could she be so lucky twice? How would she know if she didn't call soon? Tracy took a deep breath and dialed the number of Brighton Branch of the Boston Public Library, hoping as she dialed that her mother wasn't in a meeting.

"Boston Public Library, Brighton Branch, Samantha Pierce speaking."

"Samantha? Hi, this is Tracy. Is my mom around?"

"Tracy, how are you? Laura tells me she finally talked you into taking some time off. Are you still in Maine? Having a good time?"

Tracy hadn't thought of the possibility of having to talk to someone else, especially Samantha, the most loquacious person who worked in the library. Why couldn't Laura have answered the phone? Tracy didn't feel like small talk.

"I'm having a great time… still here for another week or so… Is my mom there?"

"Sure. Did you ever know her to miss or be late for work? I'll have her paged. Just a minute."

Tracy's stomach was in knots and her heart was pounding, and Samantha was telling her to wait. Waiting, which had never been one of her strong suits, was nearly impossible now. She entertained the idea of hanging up but couldn't imagine what she would tell her mother when she did finally talk to her. She waited, her nerves on edge. And waited. And waited.

"Tracy, sorry. I was interviewing a prospective new assistant librarian. How are you? I was about to call the Wentworth Cove police and have them go look for you. I was admonishing myself for telling you that to have a real vacation you'd have to keep your phone turned off. But, look at me. I'm doing all the talking. What's going on?"

"Hi, Mom. I've been pretty busy." Wanting to get straight to the reason for the call, Tracy put off telling her about Annie's letter and her jaunt up the coast. "I've been seeing Nathan a lot… I know that makes you happy… But there's something else I want to ask you about."

"What's that?"

No backing out now, Tracy. "You know that librarian at the Kennebunk library I mentioned a few days ago? I had lunch with him and Kate last week, and I got the feeling that he knows you. I don't know what it was—like I said, just a feeling… but, but a pretty strong one…" Tracy was stammering here. Deep breath. Continue. "Anyway, do you remember him? His name's John Strong." *Okay. Ball's in your court now, Mom.*

"Yes… yes, I do. As I recall he had just taken the job of librarian when I went in to get some books to help pass the time, and we talked a few times while I was in Wentworth Cove. What made you think he knew me? Did you ask him about me?"

"No. It wasn't anything he said, just the way he looked when I mentioned your name. A look of recognition. In fact, when I first met him and Kate told him I was from Boston, he had that same look. You must have made quite an impression here thirty years ago. Did someone paint a portrait of you while you were here?"

"Oh, my. I had forgotten about that. How on earth did you know about that? This is getting weird." Weird? That's not exactly what Tracy would call it. Upsetting? Disgusting? Sickening?

"Actually, Nathan's mother—I've mentioned her before. Kate."

"Yes, I remember."

"She's the one who first mentioned it. She thought I looked like the woman in a portrait that had been hanging in an art gallery here many years ago… until someone bought it, that is. Would you like to guess who that was?"

"I have no idea." *Really?*

"John Strong."

"John bought it? That's interesting."

"Interesting? You think it's interesting? What about strange? Or baffling?" An awkward silence. "Mom?"

"Tracy, I don't know what you—"

"You know what? I don't want to have this conversation right now. I'll call you later."

"Tracy, listen to me—"

Click. Tracy couldn't continue. Not now, anyway. Maybe tomorrow when her emotions were more in check. Her mom would forgive her for hanging up, probably sooner than Tracy could forgive Laura for being unfaithful to her father. The small hope that had kept bubbling up in the past was gone. What could her mom have said? Her dad was in England that summer. Laura and John were in Maine. Hot tears pooled in Tracy's eyes, and once again she was kicking herself for taking this vacation. It would have been better to never have known. But then again, what about Nathan? She wouldn't have known him either.

Ambivalent emotions swelled inside her, filling her up until she felt nauseated.

"Did I hear you talking to your mom?" Gina interrupted her thoughts. "How'd it go? Not very well, huh?"

"She didn't say as much, but her reaction when I talked about him let me know I was right about everything."

"Tracy, I'm so sorry you're having to go through all of this." Gina came over and gently put her arms around her best friend. "Is there anything I can do?"

"You've done so much already by being here with me, but this is a battle I have to fight for myself. I've never really had to forgive anyone for anything much. Catherine Carter stole my boyfriend when we were in seventh grade. I never told you about that, did I? But I forgave her because I liked her better than I liked him. Things were simple back in those days, weren't they?"

"I don't know about that. Did you forget about zits and flat chests?"

"Relatively speaking, I suppose." Gina had almost made her laugh, and they walked back into the house, arm in arm.

"You really need to give her a chance, you know. A chance to explain, if she wants to. And what about John? Do you plan to give him a chance or not? You could just walk away from here and never mention it again, but it would always be in the back of your mind. I'm right, aren't I? You can't walk away from this, can you?"

"No. No, I can't." Of course she couldn't. This revelation had toppled her world, had stripped her of the only father she'd ever known and replaced him with a man she couldn't dislike but couldn't accept either.

"What are you planning to do?"

"The girl who, three weeks ago, had her life planned down to the minute in a black leather book doesn't seem to have an answer to that question."

"All right, Tracy, let's think about it. If you can't, as you say, walk away and pretend you don't know about this at all, what's the obvious next thing you have to do?"

"I give up. Why don't you tell me?"

"You have to get to know him better, of course. You don't suppose he knows, do you?"

Tracy buried her head in her hands. "How would I know? My mother didn't seem to think it was necessary to share that information with me. Gina, what if my dad knew? I mean, he'd have to know, wouldn't he? Just because he was an English professor didn't mean he couldn't do simple math. That's something I don't think I could ever forgive her for... for hurting him like that."

"You know, Tracy, that makes me think even more highly of your dad than I did before. I mean, if he knew, and he still treated you as his own biological daughter as if nothing ever happened—well, just think about it. I never knew a father and daughter as close as you two were."

Tracy *had* been thinking about it, more than Gina knew. At the window, lace curtains followed the breeze into the room, as they had in this house for so many years while Mrs. Grayson lived here. Down the street someone mowed a lawn, the spinning whirr of the mower mocking the sounds of normalcy. Cardinals chirped and mourning doves cooed as if all was right with the world, but Tracy knew that all would not be right with her world ever again. The tears came again. She was accustomed to them now and regarded them as little more than a nuisance, but Gina hadn't seen her cry often. Tracy, the stoic. Tracy, the workaholic. Tracy, the one who didn't have time for emotion. It unnerved Gina, moved her to action.

"Look, Trace, let's shower, throw on some shorts, and go down to the beach. I haven't seen it since I came, and I think it would be good for you. You always told me the ocean held some sort of healing powers for you. Let's go try it out."

Tracy acquiesced only because Gina had come to her rescue, had left Todd and Hunter and driven over a hundred miles to help her through this crisis, and for that she was grateful. But she had no desire to go anywhere. What she really wanted to do was crawl back in bed and pull the covers over her and sleep until this feeling of betrayal went away. Yes, by her deception, Laura had betrayed her, too. She had denied Tracy the truth all these years, truth she had a right to know, truth about who her father was. Truth about who *she* was.

Chapter Twenty-One

The sun was shining brightly as they ambled down Shoreline Drive, but it didn't seem quite so radiant today. They walked the half-mile to the beach in silence and turned to take the path that Nathan and Tracy had traveled the last time they had been there together. As the sun retreated behind a cloud, transparent water streaked over stones, both large and small, and the timeless rhythm of the sea once again worked its charm on her.

Gradually, she grew calmer, all the while growing in her resolve to know the truth about John. She could never think of him as a father, that she knew, but could they forge some sort of friendship? Forgiveness would have to come first, and she remembered yet another of her father's dictums: As a worm works its way through an apple, the failure to forgive eats at the heart of the one who chooses not to forgive.

He never said it was easy, but she felt it was something she would have to do, not for her mother, not for John, but for herself, to keep this from eating at her for the rest of her life, to keep it from destroying her. She discussed it with Gina as they made their way back to the cottage, the clouds now occupying more than half the sky, the sun peeking out only occasionally.

Gina was planning to go back to Vermont in the morning, but this evening she would meet the Norsworthys. They were due at Kate's at five-thirty, and Nathan was cooking. Tracy wanted her to like them all—knew she would, really—but she was still a little apprehensive. Her best friend was meeting some people who had come to mean a great deal to her. Not only because of Nathan, but she had grown very fond of Kate, Jessica, David and Elizabeth, too. She wondered if Tim Grayson would be there. That would just about round out the people she had met in Wentworth Cove—except for Maggie and Annie, of course—but Gina had met Maggie and had been exposed, indirectly, to the evil Annie Culwell. That was more than enough.

Kate must've seen them coming up the walkway and met them at the door. "Tracy, it's been a long time since I've seen you. And this must be your friend, Gina. I'm so glad to meet you. Nathan told me you were here."

"Not much longer. I'm leaving in the morning, but I'm happy to meet you, too. Tracy has told me all about you, and that you were her first friend here."

"Tracy, I hope you don't mind, but I invited John to dinner before Nathan told me you and Gina were coming. Come in and say hi to Nathan. David and Elizabeth aren't here yet."

Tracy's heart began to pound in her chest, and she wondered if Kate could hear it. "I need to talk to you about John. I spoke with my mom this morning and… "

"Did you ask her?"

"Not in so many words, but when I mentioned his name, I could tell. Maybe not so much by what she said, but by what she didn't say."

"How are you, honey?"

"I'm as okay as I can be under the circumstances. I'm resigned and resolved. Resigned to the fact that it's true. Resolved to get to know him better and give him a chance."

"I'm glad to hear that. John is a marvelous person, probably my dearest friend in all the world." Why did there always seem to be a softness, a wistfulness, in Kate's voice when she talked about John? Could it be that she hadn't given up yet? "He isn't due until six," she continued, smiling, "so I'll have lots of time to get to know Gina better."

"Is Jessica coming with David and Elizabeth?" Tracy asked. "I had hoped Gina would get to meet her, too."

"Oh, of course, she is. Anything that is remotely connected to her uncle Nathan, Jessica will be there."

As if on cue, at the mention of his name, Nathan walked out of the kitchen and straight over to Tracy, drawing her into his arms. The sudden closeness of him, the quiet nearness of him. In his arms she felt as though she could tackle anything. *Bring on the world. I have Nathan Norsworthy.*

"Hi, Gina. Good to see you again." He let her go and hugged Gina. Gina melted, too. Tracy could tell. She knew Gina that well. She was smitten. She approved and would cease being Tracy's friend if she did anything to mess this up.

But Tracy had absolutely no intention of doing that. She was falling in love, and it was a feeling that was completely new to her—something, she realized at that moment, she'd never experienced before.

"Is anybody hungry?" Nathan interrupted her thoughts. "Mom, what time is John due?"

"Not until six, but David, Elizabeth and Jess will be here any minute."

"Can I help you with anything in the kitchen, Nathan?" Tracy asked.

"Sure. Let's go put the finishing touches on the salad. Everything else is in the oven."

As soon as they were in the kitchen, Nathan pulled her close again, holding her tightly and kissing her ardently this time, and after a while releasing her only slightly. "You didn't really think I needed help with dinner, did you?"

"You didn't really think I wanted to help cook, did you?"

"Tracy, I… This isn't a very romantic place, but I can't wait for romantic to tell you what I discovered while you were away. I love you. I love you with all of my heart, all of my being. And… and beyond that, words escape me."

"Those are the only words I need, Nathan."

"We have some things…"

"What?"

"We have some things to talk about, some things to figure out."

"Not here. Not now. What are you doing tomorrow?"

"Nothing that can't be postponed. Are you asking me for a date?"

"Could we spend the afternoon together? There's something I have to do in the morning, in Kennebunk."

He narrowed his eyes. "Something I could help you with?"

"I have to do this by myself, but I'll tell you everything tomorrow. Is two o'clock okay?"

"It will seem like fifty years," he said, planting a kiss on her forehead, "but I guess it'll have to do. I think I hear David's voice. Maybe I'd better work on the salad."

At dinner, Gina captivated everyone and John captivated Gina. Tracy guessed if the situation had been different, she would have felt the same way Gina apparently did about him. He was likable; there was no doubt about that. But she couldn't get past the fact that he had seduced a married woman, and that married woman just happened to be her mother. Tomorrow morning she would find out the truth. She didn't know how exactly, hadn't worked out the details in her mind yet, but she would find out the truth.

Chapter Twenty-Two

"Tracy, are you up?" A soft knock on the door and Kate's voice startled Tracy early the next morning as she was making coffee.

"Come in. I'm going to see John this morning. I have to know for sure."

"You might want to read this first. Bernard Solomon just brought it to me. He didn't know where to find you. Nora told him to get it to you. She thought you might like to have your mother's journal from the summer she was here. Said she thought she remembered putting some old journals that renters had left behind in the attic and had Bernard go up there and find them. This was among them. Maybe you'll find what you're looking for."

Tracy's hands trembled slightly as they reached for the book with yellowed pages. She opened it slowly, carefully, her eyes falling on the familiar handwriting.

"I'll leave so you can read it in private. Come down if you need to."

"Thanks, Kate, for everything. Gina's here. She's still asleep but plans to leave today."

With both trepidation and resolve, Tracy looked at the journal in her unsteady hands, flipped back to the first page, and started reading.

June 3

Took Ken to the airport yesterday and drove to Wentworth Cove this morning. Have settled into a room in Nora Solomon's home. She couldn't be nicer. Her home is beautifully furnished with antiques and bright floral prints. I think we will get along well, and I'm looking forward to meeting more people in this village. Will be here for two months while Ken is working on his doctorate at Oxford. Hope to get in a lot of reading and maybe a little writing. It will be quite a change from thesis research and writing. This time it's for pleasure!

June 10

It's been a week since I wrote, so I'll fill you in, Journal, on what I've been up to since that day I arrived here in the beautiful, quaint village of Wentworth Cove. The shops are wonderful, for browsing and buying. So far I've resisted everything except some cranberry candles. I can just imagine how delicious they'll smell in the fall when I'm back in Boston yearning for the Maine coast. There's a bookstore here, but I decided to borrow from the library instead of spending all my money on books.

Went to the library in Kennebunkport on Tuesday. Met the librarian, a man, which is unusual, I think. Aren't most librarians women? Anyway, it was nice to have someone to talk to who could discuss how to run a library, especially since I'll be looking for a job when we go back to Boston in August. Checked out a couple of books that John (the librarian) recommended. Started one of them and have decided that he has good taste in reading material.

June 15

The strangest thing happened yesterday. While I was walking along the coast, a man started talking to me as if he had known me all my life. I was taken aback at first, but he was so genuine and friendly that I relaxed and actually began to enjoy the conversation. Then he popped the question: "Would you mind if I painted your portrait?"

His name is Samuel Jacks, and he apparently is a well-known artist in this area. He told me that he has some works displayed at a gallery in Kennebunkport. Since I was intrigued, but a little skeptical, I drove up to see his paintings. He's quite good. I'm supposed to give him my answer tomorrow, and I really can't think of any reason not to allow him to paint me. I'll keep you posted, Journal.

June 23

Haven't written in a while, but I've been busy. What, you ask, could keep you so busy in this place where, until three weeks ago, you knew absolutely no one? Well, John—remember him, the librarian in Kennebunk?—lives in Wentworth Cove. I ran into him at the market one day, and he invited me to a party one of his friends was having. I decided to go in order to meet some people and had the best time. He's really nice, and we have so much to talk about with our common interest in books and libraries. He had some good advice for me as someone just starting out in the field.

Met John's sister at the party. Her name is Janette. She's someone I'd like to get to know better…a few years older than John…seems very protective of him…not something I can put my finger on, though. I like her personality—very outgoing and funny.

Samuel has started the painting. "On the beach," he said, "since that's where I first saw you." We've worked a little each day, except Sunday when it rained.

June 29

I don't know why I was so concerned about passing the time here for two months. It seems like yesterday that I arrived, yet it's been almost a month. Ken doesn't write as often as I had hoped, but I know he is busy with his classes.

Samuel couldn't work yesterday, so I took the opportunity to drive up the coast. Took my camera and tried to capture the beauty of the area, but I don't see how a picture of any kind could do it justice. It's simply breathtaking. Especially refreshing after all the traffic, concrete and people packed like sardines in Boston.

July 1

Went to the library again yesterday to get a new crop of books. John suggested a new writer I'd not heard of, and I'll have to admit he's one of the most talented writers I've read in a long time. John also asked me to have dinner with him tomorrow. Don't know how I feel about that, but on the other hand I don't see what harm it could do. He's so nice, and we have so much in common. Ken would like him. I know that. Anyway, I told him I'd go. It's not as if I'm going to be doing anything else. Samuel is almost finished with the portrait. Can't wait to see what it looks like. He hasn't let me see it since he started painting. Says it's bad luck.

July 2

Just got back from dinner with John. We drove into Kennebunk and ate at Sylvester's. The food was amazing! I, of course, had lobster. Only the second time I've had it since I've been here.

We talked about everything: food, books, music, family. He didn't seem to know I was married and seemed a little surprised when it came up. I just assume because I have a ring on my left hand everyone will know, but I suppose an opal is a little unusual for a wedding ring. Anyway, he knows now. I hope it won't make any difference in our friendship because he's so easy to talk to, and it helps to know someone up here.

July 7

Well, I haven't written for a while, but I guess you could say I've been too busy to think about you, Journal. No. Other things have occupied my time for a few days. You see, on July 3 at nine in the morning Nora woke me and told me I had a visitor. I couldn't imagine who it could be. Samuel is taking a little vacation, so we're not scheduled to work again until the tenth. John, I assumed, was working at the library. She said it was a young man, so I knew it wasn't Janette. I've met only a few other people here, and I didn't think any of them would come that early in the morning without calling.

It was Ken! He surprised me by coming for the long Fourth of July weekend! We had so much fun touring the area, even drove up to Camden for a day. First time I had been there since I was fourteen and went with Mom, Dad and Sara.

He left on the fifth, and I slept almost all day yesterday. We didn't sleep much while he was here. We wanted to spend as much time together as possible. It was so wonderful to be with him again. Only three more weeks and we can go home. Not that I'm that excited about getting back to Boston, but I am ready to get back to my life with Ken. This weekend reminded me how much I've missed him. Maybe we can retire here someday. Whether we do or not, I know I'll be back.

Tracy gently laid her mother's journal on the coffee table, tears welling up in her eyes, but this time they were tears of relief. Tears of joy.

How could she possibly have thought her mother would have a summer fling? But everything seemed to point in that direction.

At that moment Gina interrupted her thoughts with, "Hey, I can't believe I slept this late. Why did you let me?" She finally looked up and saw the tears streaming down Tracy's face.

"What's wrong? Did you talk to your mom again?"

"In a manner of speaking," Tracy replied, a faint smile beginning to appear on her face. When it morphed into a huge smile and Tracy broke out in laughter, Gina was more than perplexed.

"What on earth? Why are you laughing?"

"I'll let you read this while I make a phone call," she said handing the journal to Gina. "This will explain everything. Enjoy!" And she scooted away to the privacy of the bedroom.

Picking up and turning on her cell phone for the first time in several days, she dialed the familiar number. What a pleasure it was to dial it this time. So different from the last two or three times she had called her mom, not knowing what to say, not wanting to think the unthinkable as she talked to her.

"Mom? Did I call too early?"

"Of course not. 'Bout time you called your city-trapped mother again. I've tried to call you several times, but I guess your phone was turned off. Everything okay?"

"Everything's perfect. Couldn't be better. In fact, I have a proposition for you."

Chapter Twenty-Three

The first person Tracy called was Nathan. She needed help with her plan. She needed a co-conspirator, and he was her obvious first choice.

"Hi." Her voice was welcome, but he was confused. Didn't she say she had something to do this morning and would see him this afternoon?

"Hi. Are you in Kennebunk?"

"Uh, no. Change of plans. Got a minute?"

"Are you kidding? For you, I've got a lifetime."

Tracy couldn't believe her luck. Or blessing. Or whatever else you wanted to call it. She couldn't believe how much had happened in only a few weeks. Her entire world had turned inside out and upside down and back again, and she was plotting what only a day ago would have been unthinkable.

"Okay. I'll be right over. If that's okay."

"Did you say 'if'? I thought I heard you say 'if.'"

"Hey, while I'm on my way, would you be looking up flights from Boston to Portland? I don't care how much it costs. I know it's late, but I'd like one for this weekend if possible." By this time Tracy had worked out the plan in her mind and was eager to fill Nathan in on it, but wanted to tell him in person rather than over the phone.

"Sure. As long as you're not wanting me to look up flights from Portland to Boston, no problem. What's this all about?"

"You'll see. Be there soon."

It had been a long time since Tracy had been this happy, this excited about life, about the future, and her plan was heightening the excitement to the point that she was almost giddy. By the time she had arrived at Nathan's, she was practically dancing.

Nathan met her at the door, clad in his signature jeans, but this time he had on a plaid shirt. Tracy didn't think he could look any better than she'd seen him before, but there was something about that plaid shirt. He almost took her breath away. *Focus, Tracy. Remember what you're here for.*

"Hey. What's this all about? I love a good mystery, but I'm ready to be filled in on what you're up to." Of course he was. He'd been so patient over the last few days…with her up-and-down emotions, her two-day disappearance, her silence about something that was obviously bothering her.

"Did you find any good flights?"

"Not really, but I have a better idea. You want to fly your mother here, right?"

"How'd you know?"

"Lucky guess." That smile. She had trouble looking at him without melting. "Anyway, what if David picks her up? He took after my dad in wanting to get his pilot's license several years ago. He doesn't own a plane, but he could rent one."

"That's a great idea. Do you think he could pick her up Friday afternoon and take her back Sunday night?" she asked.

"I not only think it, I know it."

"You know it how?"

"I asked him."

"You asked him?"

"Yeah. I wanted to have an answer for you when you got here." Tracy couldn't believe her luck. How much better could this week get?

"All right. I'll call her and tell her to start packing. I want you to meet her. I want her to meet you and your family. And there's someone else I want her to meet. Well, she's already met him, but…"

"Who is it? Don't keep me in the dark."

"Let's pick up Gina. She has to go back to Vermont today, but I'll take you both to breakfast and tell you all about it."

The Cessna Tracy had rented and David had flown for the special mission landed in Portland at 8:10 P.M. on Friday. When Laura Ratcliffe descended the steps of the plane, seven people were there to welcome her to Maine.

Tracy introduced her first to Nathan, then Kate, David, Elizabeth and Jessica. Then Tracy glanced over at John who was grinning from ear to ear.

"Mom, I think you already know John Strong, don't you?"

"Yes. Yes, I do. John, it's been such a long time. How are you?"

John walked over to Laura and took both of her hands in his. "Great. Just great. Laura, it's so good to see you again after all these years."

"Everybody to my house for cake and coffee?" Kate asked.

"Sure, Kate. We'd love to. I can't wait for Mom to get to know all of you."

Tracy and Nathan smiled at each other as they started toward the car, and Tracy saw the promise of a future in Nathan's smile. She didn't know when or where or how, but she knew someday they would be together forever. And as she looked back at her mother, who had taken John's arm and was following a few paces behind them, she thought that somehow, just somehow, there might be two futures affected by this vacation she hadn't wanted to take.

About the Author

Rebecca Stevenson is a freelance editor and writer whose frequent visits to New England have become the inspirations and settings for her stories. She is a member of Romance Writers of America and Dallas Area Romance Authors and currently lives in Texas with her husband.

Website

http://www.rebeccastevensonwriter.com

Made in the USA
Middletown, DE
23 February 2023

25401371R00096